A PRINCESS
BY CHRISTMAS

A PRINCESS
BY CHRISTMAS

BY

JENNIFER FAYE

First published in Great Britain 2014
by Mills & Boon, an imprint of Harlequin (UK) Limited,
Large Print edition 2015
Eton House, 18-24 Paradise Road,
Richmond, Surrey, TW9 1SR

© 2014 Jennifer F. Stroka

ISBN: 978-0-263-25602-4

Harlequin (UK) Limited's policy is to use papers that are natural, renewable and recyclable products and made from wood grown in sustainable forests. The logging and manufacturing processes conform to the legal environmental regulations of the country of origin.

Printed and bound in Great Britain
by CPI Antony Rowe, Chippenham, Wiltshire

For Marcia

To the most wonderful, caring, generous lady I know. Thanks so much for being a very special part of my life. Someday when I grow up I want to be just like you.

And for Marcia's Book Crew

Thanks for all of your kind words and encouragement. You ladies are amazing!

CHAPTER ONE

AT LAST HE'D lost them.

Prince Alexandro Castanavo of the Mirraccino Islands stared out the back window of the cab as it snaked in and out of traffic. He'd never driven in New York City but his concern deepened when they swerved to the berm of the road. While all of the other traffic was at a standstill, they kept rolling along.

When the cab suddenly jerked to the left, Alex's shoulder thumped into the door. He reached for the armrest and his fingertips dug into the hard plastic. What had he done to deserve the cabbie who thought he was a grand prix driver?

Alex jerked forward as the car screeched to a halt in front of a traffic light. At least the guy obeyed some traffic rules. Another glance out the rear window revealed a bread delivery truck behind them. He breathed a sigh of relief. No one was following them. But then again, how could

they? He doubted many people drove as errati-
cally as this cabbie.

"You can let me out here?"

"No. I get you there quick."

Alex reached for his wallet, but before he could
grab it, the car lurched forward. He fell back
against the seat. What was up with this guy?
Didn't he know that he'd make more money by
taking his time?

"You don't have to hurry."

The man grinned at him in the rearview mirror. "Hurry? Sure. I hurry."

Alex inwardly groaned. He was about to correct the man when he realized that every time
the man spoke, he took his eyes off the roadway.
It was best not to distract him if Alex wanted to
reach his destination in one piece.

He silently sat in the backseat while the cabbie
jockeyed through the streets of Manhattan. Alex
stared out the side window as a fine snow began
to fall. Cars and people abounded in every direction, seemingly undisturbed by the deteriorating
weather. Garlands and festive wreaths adorned
the fronts of buildings while pine trees and shiny
ornaments decorated the shop windows. Christ-

mas was definitely in the air, even though it was still a few weeks away.

City life would definitely take a bit to get used to. Not that he planned to live it up while in town. Unlike his usual need for high visibility on behalf of the kingdom, this trip required stealth maneuvers, especially since he'd gone against protocol and stolen away without his security detail. Although in his defense, it was a necessity. Trying to elude the paparazzi was tricky enough, but doing it with an entourage would be impossible.

Soon the stores faded away, traffic thinned out and rows of houses dotted each side of the street. One last glance out the rear window assured him they hadn't been followed. At last, the tension in his neck eased.

When a loud clicking sound filled the car, he noticed they'd turned onto a cobblestone roadway. It was a narrow residential road with no parking on either side.

Alex sat up a little straighter, taking in the sweeping willow trees on either side of the street. This must be the exclusive neighborhood of Willow Heights, aptly named.

The homes in this area sat back off the road.

They were older mansions that were well kept and still stunningly beautiful. Being here was like stepping back in time. A wrought-iron sign-post came into view. It stood in front of a stone wall and read: The Willows.

Alex glanced up at the stately home with its old-world charm. He wasn't sure what he was expecting. When the problem at the palace had come to light, there had been no time for detailed planning. He'd moved directly into action. His mission was to draw out this game of cat and mouse with the press—not knowing how much time would be needed to resolve his brother's latest fiasco.

The driver turned in to the gated driveway. "That is some swanky place. You some rich muckety-muck?"

He wasn't sure what a muckety-muck was, but it didn't sound good. "No."

"You stay long?"

He wished he knew. "I'm not sure."

"When you need a ride. You call. Freddy take you."

English might be Alex's second language, but this man made him feel as if it was his first—the broken English combined with a very heavy accent left Alex struggling to understand what the cabbie was trying to say. But one thing he knew was that he wouldn't be summoning Freddy for another ride—anywhere.

The paved driveway led them to a spacious three-story flagstone mansion. By the looks of it, this place dated back a century or two. The owner certainly had done a fine job keeping up the outside. Ivy grew up one wall and its vines were dusted with snow. It didn't even come close to the enormity of his family's palace, but the large, sweeping porch draped with garlands gave the place a warm, homey feel.

The car pulled to a stop and the driver cast him a big, toothy grin. Alex reached for his credit card to pay the fare but paused. On second thought, he grabbed some cash from his wallet. It was best to keep his true identity under wraps for now.

Once he and his luggage were settled on the sidewalk, the cab raced off down the driveway. Alex's shoulders slumped as the adrenaline wore off and fatigue weighed him down. He stifled the urge to yawn. He'd never been so happy to have his feet on solid, unmoving ground; now he just had to find his room and get some shut-eye before he dropped from exhaustion.

"Welcome," chimed a sweet voice.

He turned, finding a young woman coming up along the side of the house, lugging a big cardboard box. Her reddish-brown ponytail swayed as she made her way toward him. Her beauty captivated him, from her pink-stained cheeks to her full rosy lips.

Her breath came out in small white puffs in the frigid air. Her forehead creased with lines of exertion from carrying a box that was far too big for her.

Alex sprang into action. "Let me take that for you."

She looked hesitant but then relented. "It goes on the front porch."

"Your wish is my command."

They strolled side-by-side along the walkway. She cast a curious glance his way. "Are you all right? You looked a little shook up when you got out of the cab."

"You wouldn't believe the cab ride I had here." He stopped at the bottom of the steps. "I think the cabbie drove off the road more than he drove on it."

"I take it you didn't enjoy your adventure?"

"Not at all. I am very grateful to be here in one piece. Remind me to think twice before I call that cab company again."

The young lady smiled and he found himself smiling back. This was not good. He knew better than to encourage the attention of women. It only complicated things when they wanted more than he could offer.

He forced his lips into a flat line as he moved onto the porch. The box landed with a thunk. He turned around to find the young woman standing just behind him.

As he dusted off his hands, he took in her white winter jacket with the logo for The Willows stitched in blue thread on the chest. His gaze skimmed downward, catching her snug jeans and the wheat-colored work boots that completed her ensemble. He drew his gaze up from her peekaboo curves. At last his gaze made it to her eyes— her big brown eyes. He wondered if she knew how beautiful she was. The guys must go crazy over her.

"Thank you for the help." Her gaze strayed to his luggage and back to him. "Can I help you? Are you part of the wedding party?"

"No, I'm not." His voice came out deeper than normal. "I want to check in."

"Rooms are by reservation only."

This young woman must be mistaken. "I have a reservation. Now, if you could point me in the direction of the person in charge."

The young lady pulled off a glove and held out her hand. "You're speaking to her. I'm Reese Harding. And you would be?"

He stepped closer and wrapped his cold fingers around her warm ones. Her skin was smooth and supple. He resisted the urge to stroke the back of her hand with his thumb. When his gaze caught hers, he noticed the gold flakes in her eyes.

"Allow me to introduce myself. I am P—" He caught himself just in time before blurting out his formal title. It took him a moment to recall the alias he'd used on the registration. He'd borrowed his mother's family name. "Alex De-Luca."

Then, realizing he'd held on to her hand longer than necessary, he released his hold on her.

He never let a woman affect him to this extent. Being awake more than twenty-four hours was definitely impacting him. If only he could sleep on planes, it'd help.

"You own this place?" he asked, just to make sure he understood her correctly.

"Yes, I do."

His brows gathered as he studied her. She certainly seemed awfully young to be running her own business. "If you don't mind me asking, how old are you?"

"I can assure you I'm older than I look."

Well, now she had him curious. "And that would be—"

"Twenty-five." Her dimpled chin lifted. "Don't tell me you're going to card me too?"

"Um…no." He glanced away. He was letting himself get off track. It must be jet lag, because he wasn't here to pick up women—even one as captivating as the woman standing before him. "About the room—"

"The place is full up until Monday."

"Monday?" That was impossible. The muscles in his neck and shoulders tightened. "I made the reservation for today."

"If you'd like to make another reservation, I can check our calendar." She turned and stepped inside.

He strode after her, closing the door behind him. "I assure you I have a reservation, if you'd just check."

With an audible huff, she stopped in the foyer and turned. "Listen. I don't have your reservation. In fact, I've never spoken to you in my life. I would have remembered the accent."

He would have remembered her honeyed voice, too. She was as attractive as she was frustrating. "Someone else must have taken my reservation. Surely you're not the only person who works here." Then again, this place was smaller than he'd been expecting. "Are you?"

Her forehead crinkled. "No, I'm not. But anyone you'd have spoken to would have checked the online system and known we were booked."

Not about to give up, he thought back to the phone call when he'd made the reservation. "It was a woman I spoke to about getting a room. She sounded a bit older than you. She took my information."

She frowned. "Maybe you do have a reservation. It's possible it didn't get entered in our system." She lowered her head and shook it. "But it doesn't change the fact that I don't have anywhere for you to stay. We are hosting a wedding this weekend."

He'd boarded three different flights today just to be sure he'd lost the paparazzi. And he'd suffered through a long layover in the Atlanta airport, cramped in a chair. All he wanted to do now was enjoy a warm meal and a soft bed. He held back a yawn. Rather make that a soft bed and then the warm meal. Anything else was unacceptable.

He straightened to his full six-foot-three-inch height and pressed his hands to his waist. He swallowed his frustration and strove for a professional tone. "What about my deposit?"

Her lush lips gaped and her face paled. "You made a deposit?"

"Yes. Check your computer."

Her eyes widened. "Mr. DeLuca, I'll definitely check into getting you a full refund. I'm truly sorry for the inconvenience."

He glanced around at the historic mansion. His gaze scaled up the rounded staircase, taking in the stained-glass window on the landing. There had to be room somewhere—even if it took a bit of juggling.

"Since you've already accepted my money and this place looks spacious enough, I am sure you can set up accommodations for me until this wedding is over." He flashed her one of his camera-ready smiles. "After all, I traveled a long way to get here. Now I expect you to hold up your end of the arrangement."

Her lush lips pressed into a firm line as though she were considering her options before speaking. "Why don't you follow me into the lobby while I clear up this snafu?"

Without another word the spitfire strode away. Her well-rounded hips sashayed from side to side like the metronome from the days when he'd been forced to take piano lessons. Only the swing of her backside mesmerized him in a way the silly rhythm keeper from his childhood never did. He stared at her until she disappeared back down the hallway.

Alex gave himself a mental jerk. He couldn't let himself get distracted—no matter how beautiful the distraction. He had a job to do. A mission to complete. His sole duty was to protect the crown of the Mirraccino Islands from a messy scandal—one that would most certainly rock not only the palace walls but also the entire nation.

CHAPTER TWO

REESE HARDING STRODE to the back of the man-sion, trying not to let the tall, dark stranger get under her skin. All the while, she ignored the prickling sensation at the back of her neck. Let him stare. She wasn't going to go all soft because he was drop-dead gorgeous and his mere touch made her fingers tingle.

Her gut told her that he was used to getting what he wanted—when he wanted—but it wasn't going to happen today. There honestly was no room. And by the way he could make her heart race with just a look, it was for the best.

Reese marched into the office just off the kitchen. She suspected that her mother had ac-cepted his reservation. If that were the case, Reese might very well have a legitimate prob-lem. And she'd have no one to blame but her-self. When her mother had finally come out of the dark place she had disappeared to after

Reese's father unexpectedly died, she had been so excited to see her mother's desire to help with the inn that perhaps she'd let her mother have too much freedom.

"Hey, honey." Her mother peered in from the kitchen. "What are you doing? You just tracked a trail of snow over my clean floors."

"Sorry." Reese continued rummaging through the stacks of bills and correspondence on top of the big oak desk. "I need to find something."

"Can I help?" Her mother's face lit up. "I'm feeling like my old self now and would really like to be more helpful around here. I could organize the office for you."

"Mom, we talked about this. I like it the way it is. I can usually find what I'm looking for." And she would this time, too, if Mr. DeLuca didn't have her all flustered. "Besides, we don't want to rush things. You're doing so well and all, I just don't want—"

"I know, honey." Her mother patted her back. "It's just nice to be needed. So what are you looking for?"

"There's some guy waiting in the foyer claiming to have a reservation for tonight. Do you recall taking a phone call from an Alex something or other?"

Her mother's graying head tilted to the side. "I'm not sure. A lot has been happening around here lately."

Reese stopped shuffling through the papers in the organizer and looked directly at her mother. "This is important. Think real hard. Did you take a reservation from a man with a foreign accent?"

Her mother's forehead crinkled. "When would he have called?"

"Last week." Reese grabbed another stack of papers, looking for anything that would confirm that man's words.

"Seems to me I might recall speaking to someone with a foreign accent. I remember because the connection wasn't very good."

"Really? You remember him?"

"If I took his reservation, the money will be in the computer."

Her mother was right. She was wasting her time searching through all of those papers. She could pop on the computer and confirm Alex's deposit had been made. She pushed a button to start the computer.

"I'll leave you alone to figure things out." Her mother made a beeline for the door.

Reese logged into the resort's financial account. There was indeed a deposit—a huge deposit. Surely she'd misread the amount. Even after she blinked and refocused, the same enormous dollar figure remained. Her heart picked up its pace as excitement coursed through her veins. There was more than enough cash here to rent out the entire mansion for a month.

She then checked the inn's online reservation system. There was no mention of Mr. DeLuca. How was that possible?

After some quick sleuthing, she determined that her mother had bypassed the online reservation system and taken his information over the phone manually. Oh, what a mess! She'd have to sit her mother down and have a firm talk about procedures so they could avoid these issues in the future.

Still, this influx of cash was just what they needed to pay the upcoming tax bill, not to mention the bank loan. *Calm down. You're getting ahead of yourself.*

It wasn't like she could accept his money. She

didn't have one single room to offer him. All she could do was offer Mr. Sexy Accent a full refund and hope he'd go away quietly.

But nothing about the man said he'd easily back off from what he wanted. Everything from the man's every-strand-in-its-place dark hair to his tailored white shirt that covered an obviously buff chest and down to his polished dress shoes said he was used to getting what he wanted when he wanted and the way he wanted it.

Nonetheless, she didn't have the ability to accommodate him, much less the obviously large party that he planned to host. With a weary sigh, she grabbed the checkbook to write out the refund. The pen hovered over the check and her grip tightened as she thought of turning away all of that money.

She wrote out his name and the amount. Life wasn't fair. In the past year or so, with the economic downturn, she'd had a hard time attracting people to The Willows and now she was having to turn away this obviously affluent guest because of a clerical error.

She really did feel bad for him. Then a thought occurred to her. The least she should do was help this man locate some other reasonable accommodations.

Armed with the check and her address book, she returned to the foyer. Upon finding her mother and Mr. DeLuca conversing in lowered voices, she paused by the staircase. Neither of them seemed to notice her presence. What in the world was her mother saying that was so engrossing? The man rocked back on his heels and laughed. The sound was deep and rich.

When she stepped off the carpeted runner and onto the dark, polished wood floor, her boots made a sound. Both her mother and Mr. De-Luca turned her way. Reese's hold on the sizable check tightened. It was best to get this over with quickly.

The man caught her gaze with his deep blue eyes. She was struck by their vibrant color, but beyond that they told her nothing of the man's thoughts. Talk about a poker face. What sort of things did this international hunk keep hidden from the rest of the world? And what twist of fate had brought him to her doorstep?

The rise of his brows had her averting her gaze, but not before her pulse spiked, causing her heart to flutter. Why was she so intrigued by this stranger? So what if he came from another land and had the sexiest way of rolling his *R*s? He was still just a guy and she wouldn't let herself want something that she knew could never be. Her attention needed to remain on the mansion and keeping it afloat.

"Ah, there's my daughter." Her mother leaned toward Mr. DeLuca as though they were old friends. "I'm sure she'll have cleared everything up for you. It was nice to meet you. I hope we can talk again." Her mother's eyes twinkled as a mischievous grin played across her lips.

Once they were alone, Reese pulled her shoulders back. "Mr. DeLuca, I've verified your reservation and I must apologize for the inconvenience this has caused you. My mother made a mistake when she gave you the reservation. She didn't realize that we already had a prior commitment."

The man remained silent, not appearing the least bit interested in helping her out of this awkward situation. She held out the hefty check, but he didn't make any attempt to accept it.

"This is the full amount you paid. I double-checked." When he still didn't move, she added, "The check will cover your full deposit."

"I don't want it."

"What? Of course you do. That's a lot of money."

Tired of playing word games, she stepped up to him and stuffed the check in his hand. For the second time in less than an hour, his touch caused a jolt of awareness to shock her nerve endings.

Her gaze lifted and she noticed his eyes were bloodshot, as though he'd been up all night. Then she noticed the lines bracketing his eyes and the dark shadow of beard trailing down his squared jaw. She was tempted to reach up and run her fingertips over the stubble.

She clamped her hands together. "If you'd like, I have the phone numbers of other facilities around the city that might be able to accommodate your party—"

"That won't be necessary," he said firmly. "I am staying here as arranged."

"But—"

"There are no more buts. I am staying." He pressed the check back into her hand. "And don't tell me again that there is no room. Your mother informed me otherwise."

"She did what?"

He sent her a knowing smile. "She told me there's a bedroom available. It's in some private apartment until one of the guest rooms opens up."

What in the world had gotten into her mother? Sure, she used to be impulsive back before the disaster with Reese's father, but since then she'd been so reserved, so quiet. Now she was getting active in the inn, which was great, but why in the world was she handing out her daughter's bedroom to this total stranger?

Reese shook her head, trying to dispel the image of this tall, dark, smooth-talking stranger in her bed. "She shouldn't have done that, not without talking to me."

His voice softened. "She seemed certain you wouldn't mind. After all, it's only until the other guests check out."

"But that's days away. They aren't leaving until Monday." And the apartment was so small that they'd be bumping into each other, day and... night. She swallowed hard.

At that moment, approaching footsteps sounded

on the stairs. Relieved at the interruption, Reese turned away. Sandy, in her blue-and-white maid's uniform, descended the steps with her dark brown ponytail swinging back and forth. The young woman's eyes lit up when they landed on their latest guest. It would appear that being left in the lurch by the father of her child wasn't enough to make Sandy immune to Mr. DeLuca's charming smile.

"Do you need something, Sandy?" Reese asked, hoping the girl would quit openly ogling the man.

Sandy came to a stop next to them. "I…uh… finished cleaning all of the rooms." She tore her gaze from Mr. DeLuca and turned to Reese. "Do you need anything else today? I don't mind staying longer."

"Thanks. But we're good. Enjoy your evening off."

"Um…sure. Thank you." Sandy almost tripped over her own feet as she kept glancing over her shoulder at Mr. DeLuca.

Reese turned back to him, refusing to let his tanned features, mesmerizing blue gaze and engaging smile turn her into a starstruck teenager. "Where were we?"

"We had just resolved my accommodations until the wedding party checks out. Now, if you'll show me to my room."

She pressed her lips firmly together, holding back her response until she gave it some thought. The truth was most women would probably stumble over themselves to have this hunk of a man sleep in their bed. But she wasn't most women. Men couldn't be trusted—no matter how well you thought you knew them.

But this arrangement was all about business—nothing more. What was a few nights on their old, lumpy couch? As it was, she didn't sleep all that much anymore. The concerns about meeting this month's payroll on top of the loan payment kept her tossing and turning most nights.

"I must warn you that the room is nothing special. In fact, it's rather plain."

"Is it clean?"

She nodded. The linens had just been changed that morning. "But I'm certain it won't be up to the standards you're used to or even the normal standards of The Willows. And...and—"

"And what?"

She shook her head. "Nothing important."

She couldn't bring herself to let on that it bothered her to share her tiny apartment with him. And no matter how much she reminded herself that it was business, it still felt personal having him slide between her sheets and lay his head on her pillow. Her pulse picked up its pace. Her gaze strayed to his bare ring finger before she realized her actions and refocused on a nondescript spot just over his left shoulder.

Maybe if he wasn't drop-dead gorgeous she wouldn't be overreacting. But for the first time since she'd started the inn, her hormones were standing up and taking a definite interest in a man. Not that he'd be interested in a college dropout like herself—even if quitting school hadn't been a choice but rather a necessity.

He looked pointedly at her. "If you have something else on your mind, you might as well get it out in the open now."

Heat crept up her neck as her fingers tightened around the check. No way was she confessing to her nonprofessional thoughts. "I was just concerned about where the rest of your party would be staying."

"There's no one else coming. I am the only guest."

"Just you?" Her gaze moved to the check that was now a bit wrinkled. "But this deposit covers all six rooms."

"I am a man who values his privacy."

That or he was so filthy rich that he didn't have the common sense God gave a flea. But hey, who was she to argue with some sheikh or eccentric recluse?

But the money in her hand came with some sticky strings. She'd have to open her home up to him for five days and four nights. She suddenly regretted not doing more with the upkeep of the apartment. But her limited funds had to go toward the debts her father had left as her inheritance. Soon the creditors would be calling and she wasn't sure what she would tell them.

She glanced up at the staircase and balcony with the large stained-glass window. Her mother's family had owned the mansion for generations. She didn't want to think about the tailspin her mother would go into if they had to turn this place over to the bank—not now that her mother had almost recovered from her father's deception.

So if it took bunking with this man to secure the necessary funds, she didn't see where she had much choice in the matter.

"Well, Mr. DeLuca, it looks like you've rented yourself a mansion."

What would it be like having a sexy roommate? Did he sleep in boxers? Or perhaps in the buff? And more importantly, did he walk in his sleep? Heat swirled in her chest and rushed up her neck. After all, a glimpse wouldn't hurt anyone.

The lines on the man's tanned face eased and a hint of a smile played at the corners of his full lips. "Now that we're housemates, you may call me Alex."

She wasn't so sure getting personal with him would help her roving thoughts, but she wasn't about to turn away his kindness. "And you can call me Reese."

CHAPTER THREE

THIS WAS WHERE he was to stay?

Alex followed Reese into the tiny apartment. He wondered who lived here or if it was just kept as a spare unit. Although seeing the older furniture and the coziness of the place, it didn't resemble any of the inn's photos he'd observed online. This place definitely wasn't meant for guests.

Reese swung open the door to a small bedroom. "This is where you can sleep."

He stepped up behind her in the doorway and peered over her shoulder. The decorations consisted of miniature teddy bears of all colors and designs. He'd never seen so many stuffed animals in one room. It was definitely interesting decor.

The most important feature was that it had a place for him to sleep. In the middle of the room stood a double bed sporting a royal-blue duvet with white throw pillows. Definitely nothing fancy, but at this point it didn't matter. He didn't think he could take one more step.

And to be honest, staying in these private quarters, as primitive as they were, would only make him that much harder to find. It'd been way too easy to tease the press with a juicy morsel of information about how he'd lost his heart to an American. But what no one knew was that he wanted no part of the *L* word. He'd witnessed firsthand how devastating it could be when you've lost the one person you loved with all of your heart. He refused to let himself become that vulnerable.

"Dinner is at six." Reese backed out of the doorway. "Do you need anything else?"

He stepped past her and hefted his suitcase onto the bed. "Your mother mentioned the room has a private bath."

Reese's brows rose sharply. "She was mistaken."

"I don't think so. She sounded quite certain."

Reese crossed her arms and tilted her head until their gazes met. "Well, she was mistaken, because she was talking about her room and she's not about to give it up to you or anyone."

"You seem very protective of your mother."

"She's all I've got in this world." And without another word, Reese turned and left.

Alex stood there staring at the now empty doorway, mentally comparing the image of the smiling older woman with the very serious young woman who seemed less than happy to have him here. There was a definite resemblance between the two as far as looks went, but the similarities stopped there. He rubbed the back of his neck before stretching. He was probably making too much of the first meeting. He'd see things clearer in the morning.

At last, he gave in to the urge for a great big yawn. The unpacking could wait. After being in transit for much longer than he cared to remember, it'd feel so good to lie down and rest. Just for a moment. After all, it was almost dinnertime.

He leaned his head back against the pillow. Maybe this trip wasn't going to be as bad as he'd imagined. For the time being, he could be a normal person without people looking at him with preconceived notions of what a royal should say or do. For just a bit, he'd be plain old Alex. A regular citizen. A mere tourist. Something he'd never been in his whole life.

The next morning, Alex awoke with his street clothes still on. He'd only meant to lie down for a moment. His stomach rumbled. He hadn't even made it to dinner. Then the events of the prior evening started to play in his mind.

He groaned as he recalled how in his exhausted state he'd been less than gentlemanly, demanding to have his way. He scratched at his two—or was it now a three?—day-old beard. He definitely owed Reese an apology.

After a hot shower and a much-needed shave, he started to unpack. He moved to the dresser and pulled out a drawer. He froze when he spotted a light pink lacy bra. What in the world?

His gaze moved to the right, finding a matching pair of undies. They weren't much more than a scrap of lace with a couple of pink strings. Immediately the image of Reese came to mind. This must be her bedroom. And these were her things. He slammed the drawer shut, but it was too late. His imagination had kicked into overdrive.

Not only had he been unfriendly last evening,

but he'd even stolen her bed right out from under her. He groaned. He wasn't so sure an apology was going to be enough to earn his way into her good graces.

He removed a pair of jeans and a sweater from his suitcase—the clothes he'd borrowed from his brother. They were more casual than his normal wardrobe, but this trip called for a very casual appearance. He and his fraternal twin, the Crown Prince Demetrius Castanavo, still wore the same size. Not that his brother would even notice the missing clothes, much less care about them. He had more important things on his mind at the moment.

Alex's next task was styling his temporarily darkened hair. He didn't want anyone to recognize him too soon. Let the paparazzi continue with their hunt. After all, the fun was in the chase. And it'd take them awhile to find him in this out-of-the-way inn.

As he worked the styling gel into his hair, he mulled over his brother's situation. He sympathized with Demetrius. The thought of being responsible not only for the royal family but also for an entire nation was, to say the least, a bit overwhelming. He just hoped Demetrius would come to terms with his inherited position as crown prince and not cause any further incidents—such as the potential scandal everyone was working so hard to cover up.

Next Alex added some saline drops to his eyes to refresh the colored contacts similar to the ones he'd used while he'd been on vacation a few months back. He blinked a couple of times, then inspected his image in the mirror. A smile pulled at his lips. For today, he was no longer Prince Alexandro. He was just plain, ordinary Alex. But first he had some royal business to attend to.

He stepped into the living room and heard a knock at the door. A man handed him a tray of food and Alex's mouth watered. It'd been a long time since he'd been this hungry. He thanked the man and barely got seated on the couch before he took his first big bite.

After finishing every last drop of the herb soup and devouring the turkey sandwich, he logged on to his computer. He scanned one news site and then another and another. His plan wasn't working. The paparazzi weren't following his jaunt to the U.S. the way he'd hoped they would. In fact, he'd fallen out of the headlines. This was not good. Not good at all.

He'd definitely have to up the stakes if he wanted to gain the press's fleeting attention. Uncomfortable with the idea of throwing out a juicy bit of information, he nonetheless started typing a note from a fictitious palace employee to a popular internet gossip site about his recent "activities." This was the only way to keep them from sniffing out the truth—the scandal that was his brother's life. He just wondered what lengths he'd have to go to in order to keep up this charade.

He was able to keep working into the afternoon and catch up on some important emails related to Mirraccino's shipping commerce. Once he'd pressed the send button on the last email, he made his way downstairs. He'd just found his way to the kitchen when Reese came rushing out of it carrying a stepstool. All bundled up in her coat and fuzzy pink earmuffs, she came to a halt when she noticed him blocking the hallway.

"Good afternoon." Her voice was cool and there was no hint of a smile on her face.

This would be so much easier if he hadn't

stumbled upon her skimpy undies. Even now he wondered if she had on a matching blue set. Or perhaps she preferred deep purple. Or maybe they were polka-dotted.

"Could you move aside? I was on my way out the door."

He gave himself a mental jerk. He wasn't ready for her to go—not yet. "I smell something delicious. The aroma wafted the whole way upstairs. What is it?"

She lowered the collapsible stool to the floor and leaned it against her leg. "It's homemade marinara sauce. But it's not ready yet. If you want to make yourself comfortable in the living room just off the foyer, I'll make sure someone lets you know when dinner is served."

"Do you want to join me?"

"I can't. I'm headed outside to do some work." She hefted the silver stool.

"But I wanted to speak with you."

"Can it wait? I have a couple of things I need to do before dinner."

"Of course." He kept what he hoped was an impartial expression on his face. "It's not urgent. May I help you?"

She shook her head. "I've got it."

As she headed for the front door, an uneasy feeling came over him. The ladder looked as though it'd seen far better days. Combine that with the ice and snow and it'd undoubtedly add up to trouble. Perhaps this was a way he could earn himself some points with her. But more than that, something told him Reese could use a helping hand—even if she was too stubborn to admit it.

As it was, he'd never been any good at just sitting around doing nothing. If he'd been at the palace, he'd be busy dealing with one situation or another. His country was quite involved with the exportation of its fine wines and fruit as well as being a shipping mecca. But he had to keep in mind that while he was in New York, he was plain Alex on holiday. Still, that didn't mean he had to sit around doing nothing.

He rushed off to grab his coat from the apartment. On the way back down the stairs, he happened upon a young man rushing up the steps, taking them two at a time. The guy had stress marring his face as a distinct frown pulled at his mouth. The guy grunted a hello as he rushed past. Alex couldn't help but wonder if that was the groom.

Why in the world did people put themselves through such stressful situations? He had no intention of saying *I do* any time soon—if ever. He'd seen firsthand how powerful love could be. And when it was over, it left people utterly devastated.

If he took the plunge it would be for something other than love—something worthwhile. After all, a meaningful union was what was expected of a prince. It was his duty.

Lost in his thoughts, Alex yanked open the front door. His hand grasped the brass handle on the glass storm door and pushed. At that moment, he saw Reese off to the side. The door bumped into the stool with her on it. The contraption teetered to the side. Reese jumped off just in time.

"Are you okay?" Alex rushed to her side.

"I'm fine." But she didn't look happy to see him—not that he could blame her.

"I didn't expect to find someone standing in front of the door."

"It's my fault, I should have moved over to

the side a little more, but I was having problems stringing the lights right above the door."

He glanced at them. "They look all right to me."

"Look at them from down here." She led the way into the yard, oblivious of the deepening layer of snow.

Alex followed her. When he turned back, he found she'd transformed the porch into a beautiful winter scene. There was garland lining the front of the porch. Small artificial pine trees strung with white lights stood guard on either side of the front door. And then there were strands of white twinkle lights the whole way around the porch, giving it a soft glow.

As Reese stood there puzzling over how to finish stringing the lights, her full lips pursed together. If he were impulsive—like his twin—he might consider stealing a kiss just to see if her lips were as sweet as they looked.

Alex turned to look out over the quiet street. The thought of kissing her still pulled at his thoughts. Besides probably earning him a slap for his effort, he knew kissing her was the sort of spontaneity that had gotten his brother in a world of trouble. Alex still didn't understand how the crown prince could elope with a woman he had only known for a handful of weeks. Frustration churned in Alex's gut. No one would want an impulsive ruler, including Alex himself. That's why the elopement had to be dealt with immediately and quietly without the encroachment of the press.

Alex glanced in Reese's direction to find her big brown eyes studying him. Her gaze was intense and put him off center because it was as if she could see through him—see that he was a fake. Or maybe it was his guilt from not introducing himself properly as the prince of the Mirraccino Islands that had him uneasy.

But it had to be this way. Keeping his identity hush-hush was of the utmost importance. He didn't know this woman any better than a person on the street. There was no reason to take her into his confidence and expect her to keep it. To her he was nothing more than a paying customer—end of story.

Her brow crinkled. "Is something wrong?"

"Not that I can think of."

"Okay. I just thought with you standing out

here in the cold instead of inside in the warmth that you must need something important."

This was his opening. He didn't have a lot of practice at apologies and for some reason he really wanted to get this right.

"There's something I have to say." When he had her full attention, he continued. "I am sorry about our first meeting. I was way out of line."

There was a flicker of something in her eyes, but in a blink, it was gone. "Apology accepted. But it wasn't all your fault. You were expecting a room to be waiting for you. No one could blame you for being upset."

"But then to kick you out of your own bed—"

"Don't worry. I don't sleep much anyway."

Before he could inquire about her last statement, she headed back to the porch to adjust the strand of lights on the banister.

"What do you think?" Reese returned to his side.

He didn't really notice a difference. "Looks much better."

"I don't know." She crossed her arms and studied the lights strung from one end of the porch to the other. "It's not perfect, but I guess it'll have to do."

"Do you always decorate so elaborately?"

She shrugged. "I wouldn't bother, but each home along Cobblestone Way is expected to light up their homes for the holidays."

Reese climbed on the unstable stepstool. When she swayed slightly, Alex rushed to her side.

"Let me do that for you." He held out his hands for the string of lights.

"Thanks, but I've got it. I know exactly how they go."

Instinctively he placed a hand on her hip to steady her while with his other hand he gripped the stool. The heat of her body seeped through her jeans and into his hand, sending a strange sensation pulsating up his arm.

She glanced down at him and their gazes caught for a second more than was necessary. Then she turned away and attempted to string the lights on three little hooks above the door.

"There. That should do." With his hand aiding her, she climbed down the few steps. "Would you mind plugging them in?" She pointed to the outlet on the other side of the porch.

He was glad to help, even if it was just something small. And the fact that this independent woman let him do anything at all must mean that he was making a little bit of progress with her. He liked that thought—not that he was going to let this budding friendship go too far. But it would be nice to have someone around with whom he could strike up a friendly conversation. He quickly found the end of the extension cord and plugged in the additional string of lights.

He turned around to find that she'd returned to the front lawn to inspect her own handiwork. Deciding that she had the right idea, he did the same. He glanced up at the house, finding it looked just as good as before. "You did a great job."

"It's no big deal. But it's nice to know that someone enjoys my efforts."

"Do you need help with anything else?"

"Actually, I do."

Her answer surprised him. "Tell me what you need."

"After dinner, I need to go get a Christmas tree."

She was going to chop down a tree? She might

have the determination, but he wasn't so sure that she had the physical strength. He wondered whom she would turn to if he wasn't here. The thought of her leaning on another man didn't sit well with him.

Ignoring the bothersome thought, he followed her back to the porch and helped collect her supplies. "I must admit this will be a first for me."

"Where exactly are you from?"

He didn't want to lie to her, but he knew that he couldn't be totally honest. With his accent there was no way he could pass for an American. There had to be a way around this tricky topic.

He decided to turn things around. "Where do you think I'm from?"

"I don't know." She tilted her head to the side and eyed him. "Let me think about it."

Spending time with Reese could be trickier than he'd imagined. He didn't want to lie to her, but telling her about his homeland was not an option. Maybe he should have stayed in the apartment and avoided her altogether. He inwardly groaned. As if that would be possible with them being roommates.

Besides, he already had a date with her. Correction. He had plans with her.

Oh, boy, was he in deep trouble, and it was only his second day in New York.

CHAPTER FOUR

THIS WASN'T A good idea after all.

Reese closed the side door to the garage and inhaled a steadying breath. She'd been far too aware of Alex at dinner. The deep rumble of his contagious laughter. The way his eyes crinkled at the corners when he smiled, making him even more handsome—if that was possible. And the way he listened to her as though each word she uttered truly mattered.

This was not good.

What had she been thinking inviting this man to go pick out a Christmas-tree with her? It wasn't as if she needed any help. Since her father's death, she'd been managing everything on her own. Why should that change now?

But she reasoned that Alex was an important guest. His enormous fee would help her meet this month's bills…she hoped. It was definitely a good incentive to make his stay here as pleasant as possible. And perhaps he'd recommend his friends stay at The Willows the next time they visited the city.

And if they were all as easy on the eyes, she wouldn't complain. After all, looking didn't hurt anything. It was getting involved with men that set you up for a world of pain. Just ask her mother. And even Reese had been involved with someone after her father died who'd promptly dumped her when he found out she wasn't a rich debutante. The memory still stung. How could she have been so foolish as to fall for her ex's promises?

In the end, she'd learned an important life lesson—don't trust men with your heart. Eventually they'll hurt you when you least expect it.

As for Alex DeLuca, she was so far out of that man's league that it was laughable. So what was she worrying about? She could relax and enjoy having some company for once.

She pressed the automatic garage door opener and started the truck. It coughed and sputtered and the breath caught in her throat. *Please don't let this be another thing I need money to fix.* As though in response to her silent prayer, when she turned the key again the engine caught. She exhaled a pent-up breath and put the vehicle in drive.

In no time at all, Alex was seated next to her. "Reese, thank you for allowing me to ride along."

The *R*s rolled off his tongue in such a divine way. She stopped herself just short of swooning. He could definitely say her name as often as he wanted. Realizing that she was letting her thoughts wander, she reminded herself that he was her guest—nothing else.

"Um…sure. No problem." In an effort to keep her thoughts from straying, she turned on the radio and switched stations until holiday music filled the air. As an afterthought, she said, "I hope you don't mind some music."

"Not at all. Back home my mother used to always have music filling the…house."

She noticed his use of the past tense and then the awkward pause. She wondered if he too was a member of the lost-a-parent-prematurely club. It was not something she'd wish on anyone— no matter the circumstances. But then again, maybe she was reading too much into his choice of words, as English was obviously his second language.

In an effort to change the topic of conversation to something more casual, she said, "That's right, I was supposed to guess where you're from. I'm not great with placing accents, but I'm thinking somewhere in the Mediterranean. Maybe Italy?"

"Very good guess. Maybe you are better at figuring out accents than you think."

English definitely had a different ring to it when Alex was speaking. It had a sort of soothing melody. She could listen to him talk for hours.

"If you don't mind me asking, what brought you to New York?"

"Business. Or should I say, I am between business negotiations. With people being out of the office for the holidays, I decided to stay in New York and experience a white Christmas."

"You hope."

"What?"

She could feel his gaze on her. "I meant you hope to see a white Christmas. Snow around these parts is hit or miss. The snow we're getting now might be all we get until after the New Year."

Was it possible he had no family to go home to? Why else would he rent out an inn for the holiday? Pity welled up in her. She couldn't blame him for not wanting to spend Christmas alone. She'd had a taste of that when her mother was having problems. It was lonely and sad, filled with nothing but memories.

Which led her to her next question: How did such a handsome, obviously successful man end up alone? Surely he wouldn't have a hard time finding a date or two. Oh, who was she kidding? He could probably have a different date for breakfast, lunch and dinner, seven days a week, and still have plenty leftover. Perhaps if her life were different she might have given him a chance.

Alex cleared his throat. "Are you sure we're going in the right direction? We're heading into the city."

She had been distracted by their conversation, but she couldn't imagine she'd turned the wrong way. Just to be sure, she glanced around at the landmarks. "This is the right way."

"But I thought you said we were going to cut down a Christmas tree."

"I said I was going to get one, but I never said

anything about cutting it down." She glanced over at him as he slouched down in the seat and adjusted his ball cap. "I'm sorry to disappoint you. But this is really much faster and easier for me."

"Is it much further?"

"Not far at all. In fact, we're here."

She stared out the window at the familiar city lot that was cordoned off with fencing. Pine trees ranging in size from small chubby little guys to tall slender ones littered the lot. People from old to young meandered around, pointing at this tree and that tree. Smiles covered their faces and the years rolled away as each seemed to step back in time and remember the childhood fascination of choosing their very own tree for Santa to leave presents under. If only that feeling of wonderment stayed with everyone. Instead some learned the hard way that things weren't always as they appeared. Sometimes life was nothing more than an empty illusion.

Reese's jaw tightened at the grim thought. Anxious to get this over, she said, "I'll just go check out what's available that will fit in the foyer. Feel free to look around."

"What about a tree for yourself?" When she cast him a puzzled look, he added, "You know, for the apartment?"

"I don't want one. After what happened… oh, never mind. I just don't have the time to bother."

She threw open the truck door and hopped out. She'd already circled around to the sidewalk when Alex's door opened. She noticed that he had the collar on his jacket pulled up and his hat shielded a good portion of his face. He must be cold. If he was here long enough, he'd get used to the cold weather.

He stepped up to her. "Let me know if you need any help."

"I will. Thank you."

His gaze moved up and down the walk. If she knew him better, she'd say he looked stressed. But that couldn't be the case. Who got stressed going to the Christmas tree lot? Maybe a single mom of six active little kids. Now that could be stressful. But not a single grown man.

So what was the true story? Why was Alex all alone for the holidays?

* * *

What had he been thinking to agree to come to this very public place?

Alex glanced around to see if anyone had noticed him. It was far too early in his plan to have his true identity made known. Or worse, for someone to snap a picture of him and publish it on the internet. He pulled his ball cap a little lower. Sure, he had his disguise in place, but he knew that it would not hold up under the close scrutiny of the press's cameras.

He slouched a bit more and avoided making eye contact with anyone. Fortunately no one seemed to pay him the least bit of attention. The people meandering about seemed more interested in finding the perfect Christmas tree than the couple of dozen other shoppers.

Thousands of holiday lights were strung overhead. This town certainly had a thing for lights, from the little twinkle ones to big flashing signs. He gazed at the trees, wondering what it'd be like to be here with his own family choosing the perfect tree—not that he had any immediate plans for a family. He knew a proper marriage was expected of him, but the thought didn't appeal to him. His duty was to look after his father, the king.

After all, if it wasn't for him, his mother, the queen, wouldn't have been shot by a subversive. The poignant memory of his mother taking a bullet in the chest brought Alex up short. Because of one thoughtless act, he'd devastated lives, leaving his father brokenhearted and alone to shoulder the weight of Mirraccino's problems.

That long-ago day was still fresh in Alex's mind. He'd grown up overnight and learned the importance of rules and duty. He didn't have the luxury to wonder what his life might be like if he were an ordinary citizen. He was a prince and with that came duties that could not be shirked—the consequences were too much to bear.

Still, that didn't mean he should forgo his manners. And thanking Reese for her hospitality would be the proper thing to do. He stopped in front of a chubby little tree that would look perfect in the apartment. It'd certainly cheer the place up.

A young man with a Santa hat and red apron approached him. "Can I help you?"

"I'd like to buy the little tree in the corner."

The guy eyed him up as though wondering why he'd want something so tiny. The man rattled off a price and Alex handed over the money.

With the little tree stowed in the back of the pickup, Alex sought out his beautiful hostess, who was pointing out a tall, slender tree to an older man with a white beard. His cheeks were chubby and when he laughed his round belly shook. Alex wondered how many times children had mistaken him for Santa. Even the man's eyes twinkled when he smiled.

The man glanced at Alex before turning back to Reese. "This must be your other half. You two make a fine-looking couple. Is this your first Christmas together?"

"We're not together." Reese's cheeks filled with color. "I mean, we're not a couple. We're...um—"

"Friends," Alex supplied.

Although on second thought, the man's observation did have some merit. In fact, the more he thought of it, the more he wondered if the man was on to something. Reese would make any man the perfect girlfriend.

She was certainly beautiful enough. When she smiled, she beamed. And in the short time he'd known her, he'd gotten a glimpse of her strength and determination.

She'd make the ideal fake girlfriend.

After all, he was supposed to be in the States because of a love interest. And with the speed with which he'd had to put this plan in motion, he hadn't had a chance to find someone to fill the role. But if the need arose, would Reese be willing to play along?

Something told him that with some gentle persuasion, she could be brought round to his way of thinking. Okay, maybe it was more a hope than a feeling. But for now none of that mattered. Hopefully his brother's rushed marriage would be resolved quickly and quietly so that involving Reese wouldn't be necessary. But it never hurt to be prepared. His father's motto was Hope for the Best, But Be Prepared for the Worst.

Perhaps Alex should do a little research and see what challenges he would be up against with Reese. He'd probe the subject with her when they were alone in the truck.

Alex leaned over to Reese. "You found a tree?"

"Yes, I did. I think it'll be perfect." She pointed to the tree the man inserted into a noisy machine. Alex watched as the tree's limbs were compressed and bound with rope.

"It'll make a great Christmas tree. You have good taste."

Reese turned to him and smiled. Such a simple gesture, and yet his breath hitched and he couldn't glance away. Big, fluffy snowflakes fluttered and fell all around them. And the twinkle lights reflected in her eyes, making them glitter like gemstones.

"As soon as they bundle it up we can go home." She moved as if to retrieve the tree, breaking the spell she'd cast over him.

Alex, at last gathering his wits, stepped forward. "I'll get it."

She frowned as though she were about to argue, but then she surprised him by saying, "Okay."

With the tree secured in the bed of the truck, Alex climbed in the heated cab. He rubbed his hands together. "I remembered everything for this outing except my gloves."

Reese's face creased with worry lines. "You should have said something. Here, let me crank up the heat."

"Not necessary. The sting from the pine needles is worse than the cold."

"Let me know if you need anything when we get back to the house. Antiseptic cream, maybe?"

"I will." This was his chance to broach the subject in the forefront of his mind. "What did you think of Santa back there mistaking us for a happy couple?"

"That he needs a new pair of glasses."

"Surely being my girlfriend wouldn't be so bad, would it?"

Once stopped at a red light, Reese gave him a long look.

He started to feel a bit paranoid, as though he had a piece of lettuce in his teeth or something. "What?"

"I'm just looking for some sign that you hit your head when you were swinging that tree around."

"Very funny." When she smiled, a funny sensation filled his chest. "You still haven't answered my question. Would I make good boyfriend material?"

She jerked her gaze forward just as the light changed. "You can't be serious. We—we don't even know each other. And I'm not looking for a relationship. Not with you. Not with anybody."

"Understood." He was at last breaking through her calm reserve. He couldn't push her too hard too fast. "I was just hoping your rejection of the idea of us being a couple wasn't a personal one. After all, I showered and shaved today. My clothes are clean," he teased. "And I carried that great big tree for you."

"That's the best you can come up with?" She smiled and his breathing did that funny little tickle thing at the back of his throat again.

"Pretty much. So if circumstances were different, would I stand a chance with you?"

"I'll give you this much, you are persistent."

"Or maybe I'm a glutton for punishment." He sent her a pleading look.

"And I'm sure those puppy eyes work on all of the ladies, don't they?"

He sat up a little straighter. "Is it working now?"

The chime of laughter filled the truck. "If you aren't a salesman, you certainly missed your calling."

Did that mean he'd sold her on the idea that he was worthy of a second or third look? He didn't know why her answer had suddenly become so important to him. It wasn't as though this part of his plan had to be implemented—yet.

Still, he found himself enjoying the smile on her face. It lit up the night. She should definitely do it more often.

Reese tramped the brakes a bit hard for a red light, jerking him against the seat belt. "I'm sure you'll make some lucky lady the perfect boyfriend."

It was his turn to smile. "Thanks for the ringing endorsement. What would it take to tempt you to play the part?"

"Of what? Your girlfriend?"

In for a penny, in for a pound. "Yes."

She laughed. "Fine. If you must know, if by chance I was looking—which I'm not, but if I were—you might have a chance. But I seriously don't have the time…if I was interested."

"Ouch."

"Is it your hands?"

"No. It was my ego. It just took a direct hit."

She shook her head and smiled. "I'm sure you'll survive."

He leaned back in the seat as she skillfully

guided them homeward. With Reese behind the wheel, Alex relaxed enough to let his thoughts wander.

How was it that someone so beautiful and entertaining could be single? Surely she wouldn't be alone for long. The image of Reese in someone else's arms took shape in his mind and with a mental jerk, he dismissed the unsettling idea. Her future relationships were none of his business. Period.

CHAPTER FIVE

PEACE AND QUIET at last.

Reese smiled to herself. The wedding party was off for the rehearsal and dinner. They wouldn't be home until late. She'd even let the staff go early. After all, it was the holiday season and there was nothing here that she couldn't manage on her own. And her mother was upstairs watching her favorite crime drama.

"Reese?" Alex's deep voice echoed down the hallway.

"In here." She was kneeling on the floor, sorting strands of twinkle lights.

He stepped into the room. "What are you doing?"

"Trying to get these lights to work. I need to replace the lightbulbs—one by one. Someday I'll have to buy new strings, but not this year." They would light up—even if she had to sit here all night exchanging the little bulbs. "What do you need?"

"I finished with my work and wondered if I could lend you a hand."

"You spend a lot of time on your computer, don't you?"

"It's a portable office. It allows me to work from anywhere."

She pulled out another bulb and replaced it with one she was certain worked. Still the strand remained dark. "So this isn't a holiday for you?"

"I would rather keep busy. I am not good at sitting around doing nothing." He knelt down beside her. "Let me have a try."

She glanced at him, surprised anyone would voluntarily offer to fix Christmas lights. Before he had a chance to change his mind, she held out the strand to him. "Good luck."

He moved closer. His warm fingers brushed over hers. His touch lingered, sending an electrical current up her arm. The reaction frazzled her common sense. She stared into his eyes as her heart pounded in her ears. He was the first to turn away. A sense of disappointment plagued her.

Regaining her senses, she jumped to her feet.

She took a step back, hoping to keep her wits about her. She'd been avoiding him since that awkward moment with Santa—er, that man at the tree lot. Why the man had assumed they were a couple was beyond her. It wasn't as if she looked at Alex with dreamy eyes. Okay, so maybe she just had. But it was just for a moment. And it wasn't as if she was truly interested in him.

But then Alex had continued the conversation in the truck. What was that all about? She still wasn't certain if he had just been joking around or if he'd been hitting on her. At least she'd set him straight—a relationship wasn't in her plans. She refused to be lied to by another man.

Alex pushed a small lightbulb into the socket. Nothing lit up. "I don't smell any food cooking. That's a first. This place always has the most delicious aromas."

In that moment, she realized in her exuberance to let everyone have the evening off that she hadn't thought about dinner. And she didn't have a good history with the stove. Anything she put near it burned—to a crisp.

"I'm afraid that I let the staff have the evening off. With the wedding party gone for the evening and the holidays approaching, I thought they would enjoy some time off. So I'm not sure what to do for dinner, as I'm an utter disaster in the kitchen."

"It doesn't have to be anything fancy. In fact, simple sounds good."

Against her better judgment, she was starting to like this guy. "How simple were you thinking? I can work the microwave, but that's about it."

His brow arched as amusement danced in his eyes.

"Hey, don't look at me like that. A person can't be good at everything. So how about a frozen dinner?"

His tanned nose curled up. "Or we could order a pizza?" He loosened a bulb from the strand. "They do deliver here, don't they?"

She nodded. "I'll check to see if my mother will join us. I'll be right back with the menus."

She rushed out of the room and up the stairs to the little apartment that she'd been sharing with her mother since her father's death two years ago, when her life had changed from that of a carefree college student with the whole world ahead of her to a college dropout, striving to keep a roof over her brokenhearted mother's head.

Not that she would have ever made any other choice. Her mother had always been there for her—she'd made her smile and wiped her tears. Now it was Reese's turn to pitch in and help. That's what families did—took care of each other.

"Hey, Mom," Reese called out, bursting through the door of their apartment. "How do you feel about—"

The words died in her throat as she noticed her mother sitting before a tiny Christmas tree on the coffee table. It was lit up and had a few ornaments on it. What in the world? Where had it come from?

Her mother was staring at it as if she were lost in her thoughts. Was she thinking about the past? Was her mother remembering how Reese used to beg her father for her very own Christmas tree?

The memories Reese had been suppressing for so long came rushing back. The image of her father's joyful smile as he held a tiny pine tree in his hand had her chest tightening. Back then he'd call her his little princess, and she'd thought the sun rose and set around him. How very wrong she'd been.

"Mom?" Her voice croaked. She swallowed hard and stepped closer to her mother. "Are you okay?"

Her mother blinked and glanced up at her. "I'm fine. But I'm glad you're here. I just had a phone call and your aunt isn't doing well."

Relieved to find that her mother wasn't sinking back into that miserable black hole where she seemed virtually unreachable, Reese asked, "What's wrong with Aunt Min?"

"She's having a hard time adjusting since Uncle Roger passed on. That was her neighbor and she agreed to come pick me up. I know with the holiday approaching and the wedding this weekend that this is the wrong time to be leaving you alone, but no one knows your aunt as well as me."

Reese wasn't so sure about her mother leaving to comfort someone who was grieving. She knew for a fact it was not an easy position to be in. But her mother appeared to be determined, and she supposed there was nothing she could say to change her mind.

"What can I do for you?" Reese asked, ready to pitch in.

"Absolutely nothing. You already have your hands full here." Her mother gave her a hug. "I've got to pack before my ride gets here."

Her mother was headed for the bedroom when Reese called out, "Mom, where did the tree come from?"

"Alex. He thought you might like it."

Her mother disappeared into her bedroom and Reese turned. The long-forgotten handmade ornaments on the little tree caught her eye.

Well, if he was so interested in having a Christmas tree, he could have it in his room—er, her room. She unplugged the lights, carried the tree to the bedroom and pushed aside her collection of miniature teddy bears—some that were as old as she was and some that were antiques collected from her grandmother and yard sales.

She'd always planned to update the room, but once she'd formally withdrawn from college, she'd packed up her apartment and put everything in storage. There wasn't time to worry about knickknacks when there was an entire inn to run. And now she was just too tired after working and smiling at the guests all day to be worried about redecorating a room where she barely spent any time.

She glanced at the bed with its comforter haphazardly pulled up. She imagined Alex sleeping in it. There was something so intimate about knowing that the Mediterranean hunk was sprawled out in her bed. Just as quickly as the thought came to her, she vanquished it.

He was a man—not to be trusted. And he'd only gone and confirmed her thoughts when he went against her wishes with the little Christmas tree—even if it had been an effort to be considerate. Conflicting emotions churned in her stomach. Why couldn't he leave well enough alone?

Not needing or wanting the aggravation, she pulled the door closed on the room. And that's exactly what she needed to do with Alex—close the door on this thing that was bubbling just beneath the surface.

He'd put this off long enough.

Alex retrieved his phone from his pocket. It was time to let the king know that he was safe. In return, hopefully he would have good news as well. Perhaps this mess with his brother, the crown prince, had been quietly resolved. Then Alex could pack his bags and catch the first flight home—away from his beautiful hostess, who muddled his thoughts and had him losing focus on his priorities.

He dialed the king's private line. The phone was answered on the first ring, as though his papa had been sitting there waiting for him to call.

"Papa, it's me, Alexandro."

"At last, you remember to call."

"I had to move quickly and quietly in order to elude the paparazzi."

"Tell me where you are so I can dispatch your security detail."

"No." Alex's body tensed as he envisioned the dark expression settling over his papa's distinct features. It wasn't often that someone said no to the king. In fact, this was the first time Alex had done it since he was an unruly child. "I have to do this. It's the only way to protect the family. If your enemies learn of Demetrius's rash actions, they'll make it a public scandal by painting him as unfit to rule. They'll gain more support for their planned takeover."

"That's not for you to worry about. The royal cabinet has that under control."

He wanted to believe his papa's comforting words, but Alex had his own sources and they all told him that these subversives meant business. He knew that no matter how old he got, his papa would still try to shield him from the harsh realities of life. But now wasn't the time for being protective. There'd already been one uprising that year. They couldn't risk another.

"I understand, Papa. But trust me when I say I have to do this. It's for the best. As long as the press is curious of my activities, they'll focus on me instead of sniffing around the palace for a piece of juicy gossip."

The king let out a long, weary sigh. "I'll admit that it has been helpful. So far only the necessary staff know of this debacle. The councillor seems to think we should be able to clear this up soon… if only your brother would come to his senses."

"You're still opposed to this marriage?"

"In these uncertain times, we need a strong liaison with one of our allies." There was a strained pause. "If only this girl had some important connections."

His papa sounded much older than he'd ever heard him before. Alex's gut knotted with frustration. When was his older twin ever going to learn that he had responsibilities to the crown, the kingdom and to their papa, who would never step down from the throne until he was secure in the fact that his successor was up to the challenge of safeguarding the kingdom. His father had never rebounded fully after the queen's death. And now his health was waning.

Alex recalled how he'd made it to her side as she drew in her last breaths. Pain arrowed through his chest. She'd told him to take care of his papa. He'd promised to do it. And that's what he'd been striving to do ever since. Not that anything he did could make up for his part in his mother's death.

"Don't worry, Papa. I know what I'm doing."

Alex's thoughts strayed back to their visit to the Christmas tree lot.

You two make a fine-looking couple.

The more he thought of Santa's words, the more he was certain he was right—Reese had the right beauty and poise to pull off the plan he had in mind. Perhaps it was time he started figuring out ways to fit Reese into his agenda.

"Papa, everything will work out. When the time is right, I'll call for my security detail."

There was another pause. He wondered if the king was debating whether or not to command he change his plans and return home immediately.

"Alex?" The sound of Reese's voice trailed down the hallway.

"Papa, I must go. I'll call again soon." And with that he disconnected the call and switched off his phone. "I'm coming." He reached for the cabinet next to the sink, searching for a glass.

"Oh, here you are. I thought maybe you changed your mind about dinner and decided to cook instead."

"I don't cook, either. I just got thirsty." And he truly was thirsty after tap-dancing around, trying to pacify his papa.

After he downed a glassful of water and set it aside, he turned to her. "What did you need?"

"I ran upstairs to get these." She held up an array of menus.

She'd been in the apartment and that meant she

must have noticed the little Christmas tree that he'd decorated to cheer up the place. Her mother had supplied some old ornaments. So why hadn't Reese mentioned it?

"Here." She stepped closer with her hand outstretched. "Pick your favorite."

He waved her away. "You pick. Whatever you choose will be fine."

Her gaze didn't meet his. "Are you sure?"

He nodded. He'd made enough decisions for tonight. He didn't feel like making any more, even if it was something as simple as pizza. In some ways, he used to envy his brother for being the crown prince, with the way people looked up to him. But as Alex got older, he was relieved to have been delivered second. It was very stressful and tiring making decisions day in and day out that impacted so many people.

Sure, to the world being royalty was all glamour and five-star dinners and balls. But behind palace walls in the executive suite there were heated debates, and the newspapers were quite critical of the decisions made by the monarchy. There was no way to please everyone all of the time.

But in this one instance, Alex was needed to keep the Mirraccino Islands together and peaceful. He would do whatever it took to keep the paparazzi from finding out the truth. Because he knew all too well what happened when a royal forgot his allegiance to the kingdom—the price was much too dear.

He cleared the lump in his throat. "While you call in the order, I can set up the tree in the living room."

"Did you get the lights to work?"

"Yes, I did. It was one bulb that was burned out. I replaced it and at last, there was light."

"Thank you." Her tone held no warmth. "Um, about the tree…I usually set it up over there next to the staircase. But I can do that myself—"

"Consider it done."

"I thought maybe you'd be tired of decorating."

So she had noticed the little tree. And it didn't seem as though she was pleased. Sure, she'd told him not to bother, but he'd thought she was too busy to do it herself and would enjoy the surprise. Her cool demeanor told him that her reason for not wanting a tree went much deeper than that.

"Christmas is one of my favorite holidays." He wondered if maybe she'd open up a little.

"That's nice." Her frosty tone chilled him. "I put the boxes of decorations next to it."

"You'll need to show me. I don't know how you want it decorated."

"Oh, that's easy. I always start with the white twinkle lights. Then I add gold ribbon and red glass ornaments."

"Do you trim the tree by yourself?"

"Yes. I find it is easier. I know how it should look, so why bother explaining how I want it when I can just as easily do it myself? In fact, you don't need to bother with it. I'll just place this call and be right back."

Reese strode out of the room like a woman on a mission. He thought it was sad that she insisted on doing so much around this place by herself. It sounded very lonely. Well, this Christmas would be different. He walked over to the tree and moved it to a spot next to the steps.

This Christmas he'd help her find the joy of the holiday.

CHAPTER SIX

WHY DIDN'T HE listen to her?

Reese frowned when she returned to the foyer. Alex was busy stringing the lights. And he didn't have the tree in the right spot. She usually moved it a little closer to the stairs to keep it out of the way. She knew she was being picky. She'd known for a long time that it was one of her faults. But things must be in their proper place or it drove her to distraction.

Alex turned to her. "I went ahead and started."

She nodded, trying to not let it bother her that the tree was out of place. Or that the lights needed to be redone if they were going to make it the whole way to the top.

"You don't like it?"

She knew that he'd tried his best and she really did appreciate it. She shifted her weight from one foot to the other and continued holding her tongue. Why did it have to bother her so much? She was being silly.

"What is it?" His eyes beseeched her.

She let out a pent-up breath. "The tree needs to be moved back out of the way."

"I know. But it is easier to decorate it here."

"And the lights, they need to be spread out a little more or you'll run out before you get to the top."

He arched an eyebrow. "You can try to get me to quit, but I won't. I'm going to help you decorate this tree."

"You're stubborn."

"And you're picky."

"Something tells me we have that in common." She could give as good as she got.

He smiled. "Maybe I am. But I know what I like."

His gaze was directly on her as he stepped closer. Her heart shot into her throat, cutting off her breath. His gaze dipped to her mouth before returning to meet her curious stare.

"You're very beautiful." The backs of his fingers brushed her cheek.

She should move, but her feet wouldn't cooperate. Shivers of excitement raced down her neck and arms, leaving goose bumps in their wake. She stared into his mesmerizing blue eyes, drowning in their depths. It'd been so long since a man had been interested in her. And she hadn't realized until now how lonely she'd become. After Josh—

The memory of her ex jarred her to her senses. She stepped back. This couldn't happen. She'd promised herself that she'd keep men at a safe distance.

Alex's hand lowered to his side. If she didn't know better, she'd say there was a flicker of remorse in his eyes. What should she say to him? After all, he wasn't Josh. Her ex had been needy and demanding. Alex was thoughtful and understanding. They were opposites in almost everything. So why was she backing away? After all, he'd soon be moving on and returning to his home—far away.

Maybe she shouldn't have backed away. Maybe she should have satisfied her curiosity to see if his kisses were as passionate as she imagined them in her dreams.

But the moment had passed. There was no recapturing it. She moved to the tree and knelt down to start adjusting the string of lights.

"Could you help me on the other side of the tree?" She tried to act as though the moment hadn't shaken her.

"Just tell me what you need me to do."

To Alex's credit, he let the awkward moment pass without question. By the time they moved the decorated tree into the correct position, Reese had to admit that she'd enjoyed her evening. Alex was actually quite entertaining with his various bits of trivia. Who would have guessed it?

It wasn't until after the wedding guests streamed through the front door that she was able to lock up the house. She climbed the steps to the tiny apartment, anxious to call it a night. She was just about to close the door when she heard footsteps bounding up the stairs. She didn't need two guesses to know that the heavy footsteps didn't belong to the anxious bride across the hall or one of her smiling attendants. No, it was the one man who got under her skin. She thought of rushing off to her mother's bedroom, but she felt the need to thank him for making a chore that normally came with some harsh, painful memories into a pleasant experience.

She turned to him. Her gaze settled on his lips. The memory of their almost kiss sent her stomach spiraling. "I—I'm heading to bed. I just wanted to thank you for the help tonight. If it wasn't for you, I would still be working at it."

"You're welcome. And it turned out well, even if it isn't exactly how you normally do it." His brows drew together as his gaze swept around the room. "What happened to the little Christmas tree?"

"I moved it to your room. I thought you could appreciate it better in there."

"But I did it for you."

"And I told you that I didn't want a tree."

"But the tree downstairs—"

"Is the price of doing business. Guests expect an inn to be decked out for the holidays, and it's my job to fulfill those expectations. But that doesn't mean I have to decorate my personal space."

"I was only trying to help."

"That's not the type of help I need." The words were out before she could stop them. Exhaustion and worry had combined, causing her thoughts to slip past her lips. "I'm sorry. I didn't mean to snap at you."

He shook his head. "You're right. I thought— ah, it doesn't matter what I thought."

The hurt look in his eyes had her scrambling for an explanation. "It's just that Christmas brings back bad memories for me and my mother. And I'm afraid that it'll upset her. I'll do anything to keep her from going back to that lonely dark place where she went after my father died."

He eyed her up as though he were privy to her most private thoughts. "Your mother seems like a strong lady. Perhaps she's stronger than you think."

Reese shook her head, recalling how her mother had crumbled after learning that her father had been on his way to his mistress when he'd died in a car accident on Christmas Eve. Loss and betrayal combined to create the perfect storm to level her mother—a woman she'd always admired for her strength. It had brought her mother to her knees and Reese never wanted to witness anything so traumatic again.

Reese pressed her hands to her hips. "You don't know her like I do."

"That's true. But sometimes an outsider can see things someone too close to the situation will miss."

She lifted her chin. "And what exactly have I missed?"

"Did you know it was your mother who got out the Christmas decorations for me to use on the little tree?"

"You must have pressured her. She wouldn't have voluntarily gotten those out. Those were... were our family ornaments, collected over the years."

"Actually, it was her idea. She insisted I decorate it for you. She thought it would make you happy."

No, that wasn't possible. Was it? Reese took a step back. When the back of her knee bumped into the couch, she sat down. What did this mean? Had she been so busy that she'd missed seeing that her mother truly was back to being herself?

"I had no idea it would upset you so much."

"It's just that...that my father always made Christmas such a big affair. It's hard to think of it and not think of him." But she failed to add the most painful part. She couldn't bring herself to admit that her father had left them on Christmas Eve for another woman. And he'd spent their money on that woman…buying her a house and leaving them in debt.

Alex stepped forward and took a seat beside her. "I didn't know."

"My mother didn't mention it?"

"She said that it has been awhile since you two celebrated Christmas, and she thought it was time you both had a good one."

Reese's heart filled with an unexpected joy. "She really said that?"

He nodded. "Otherwise I wouldn't have gone through with decorating the tree without your approval."

If this was okay with her mother, who was she to disapprove? Maybe it hadn't just been her mother who'd been deeply affected by her father's actions. In the past couple of years, Reese had been so busy worrying about keeping a roof over their heads that she hadn't realized how much her father's actions had hurt her. Or how she'd let her father steal the magic of the holiday from her.

Reese turned to Alex. "I'm sorry I was so grinchy about it."

"Grinchy?"

"Yeah, you know the story, *How the Grinch Stole Christmas?*"

"I'm not familiar with it."

"I didn't think there was anyone who didn't know that story. You must have lived a sheltered life."

"I had books, but they were educational."

"Like I said, you lived a sheltered life. Don't worry. I'm sure we can find you a copy somewhere and broaden your horizons."

"My horizons are plenty broad," he protested. "Would you mind if I brought the tree back out here?"

"Suit yourself." She most certainly wasn't the only one used to having her way.

As he strode away, she wondered why it had taken a total stranger from another land to open her eyes and help her see her life more clearly. It was as if she'd been living with tunnel vision these past couple of years, focusing on protecting her mother from further pain and keeping their home.

And though Alex was certainly a nice distraction, she couldn't let herself lose focus now. The Willows was far from being out of debt. In fact, even with Alex's generous fee she still might have to let go of Sandy, the maid and a single mom. The thought pinched at her heart.

With it being Christmas, surely there would be a miracle or something. It wasn't as though she was really a grinch, but if she had to eliminate Sandy's position at Christmastime, the comparison with that fictional character would hit far too close to home—heartless.

"Here we go." Alex strode back into the room.

She noticed how when he entered a room, his presence commanded attention. She wasn't sure what it was about him that gave her that impression. It could be his good looks or his six-foot-plus height. But no. It went beyond that. It was something much more significant, but she just couldn't put her finger on it. Maybe it was the way he carried himself, with a straight spine and level shoulders. Or the way he had that knowing look in his blue eyes. She sighed in frustration, unable to nail down exactly what was so different about him.

Alex paused. "Did you change your mind?"

"Oh, no. I guess I'm more tired than I'd originally thought."

"After I plug in this cord, would you mind turning out the lights? There's nothing like the glow of a Christmas tree."

She got to her feet and moved to the switch.

When the colored bulbs lit up the chubby little tree that to Reese resembled nothing more than a branch, she doused the overhead light. But it wasn't the tree that caught and held her attention. It was the look on Alex's face. For a second, it was the marvel of a little boy staring at a Christmas tree for the first time.

"Isn't your Christmas tree like this?" She was genuinely curious.

He shook his head. "It's quite tall and it's more formal, similar to the one you have downstairs."

"You mean it doesn't have candy canes and little bell and penguin ornaments?"

Again he shook his head. "No. Everything has to be picture-perfect. The way my mother would have wanted it."

A little voice in the back of her mind said to let the comment pass, but she couldn't. She wanted to know more about him. Maybe if she demystified him, he'd have less of a hold on her thoughts.

"Your mother...did you lose her?"

The words hung heavy in the air.

At last, Alex nodded. "She died when I was a teenager. Christmas was her favorite holiday. In fact, Papa still has the—the house decorated like she used to do. On Christmas Eve, for just a moment, it's like she's still there and going to step into the living room at any moment."

"It's good that you have such happy memories to hold on to."

"Enough about me. I'm sure you have special memories of the holidays."

She waved away his comment. "They aren't worth getting into."

She wished she could concentrate on the good times, but her father's betrayal had smeared and practically obliterated them. In her mind, that man was not worth remembering. Not after what he'd done to them. She stuffed the memories to the back of her mind.

This was why she no longer enjoyed the holidays—they dredged up unwanted memories. She wished she had nothing but good memories, like Alex. She envied him.

"I'm going to sleep." Not that she'd close her eyes any time soon. "Would you mind turning out the lights before you go to bed?"

"Not a problem." He smiled at her and her stomach fluttered. "But before you go, there's one other thing."

With nothing but the gentle glow of the little tree filling the room, it was far too romantic. Her gaze returned to his lips. They looked smooth and soft. She wondered what it'd be like to meet up with him under the mistletoe. Realizing she'd hung some downstairs for the bride and groom to indulge in, she wished she'd saved some for up here.

Alex cleared his throat. As her gaze rose to meet his, amusement danced in his eyes. Surely he didn't have a clue what she'd been thinking. Did he?

"What were you saying?" She struggled to do her best to sound normal and not let on that her heart was racing faster than the hooves of the horses who pulled the carriages around Central Park.

"I don't want to embarrass you, but did you know you have a leak in your roof?"

She nodded. "I had it fixed last week. I just haven't gotten around to getting the interior repaired."

"I could take a look at it. If you want."

She shook her head. "You're a paying guest. Not hired help."

"But I am volunteering."

Why did he always have to push? Well, this time he wasn't getting his way. "I don't need your help."

He stared at her long and hard as though trying to get her to change her mind. "Understood. I'll see you tomorrow."

At last she'd gotten through to him. "Good night."

She turned and headed back down the hall. She could sense his gaze following her, but she refused to glance back. He created a mixed-up ball of emotions in her that constantly kept her off kilter.

And what unsettled her the most was the fact that she liked him. No matter how much he pushed and prodded her, beneath it all he was genuinely a nice guy. Although he was awfully tight-lipped about his past and his family. She noticed how every time he started to mention a piece of his life, he clammed up. What was that all about?

Time passed quickly. In no time at all, Alex moved across the hall to the executive suite. He was amazed by how hard Reese worked every single day, from the time she got up before the sun until she dropped into bed late at night. He soon found himself bored of the internet, even though his leaked letter to the paparazzi had worked as he'd hoped. Now the gossip sites were filled with all sorts of outlandish stories, but the most important part was that they were looking for him. He just had to keep his disguise in place a little longer.

He thought of Reese and how she'd react upon learning he was a prince. Somehow he couldn't imagine she'd treat him any different if she knew the truth. Or was it that he didn't want her to treat him different? He liked their budding friendship—in fact, he liked it very much.

Guilt plagued him for not being more open with

her. She'd been kind and generous with him—he wanted to treat her with the same sort of respect. He considered telling her everything, but in the next thought he recalled how deviating from the plan had cost his mother her life.

Alex paced back and forth in his suite. It was best for everyone to keep up the pretense of being a businessman—which he truly was back in Mirraccino. What he needed now was something to keep him busy.

It was still early in the morning when he strode across the hall to Reese's apartment and rapped his knuckles firmly on the dark wood door. No answer. After having lived with her for the past few days, he didn't think anything of trying the doorknob. When it opened, he stepped inside.

"Reese, are you here?"

Again, no answer.

He glanced around, pleased to find that the little tree was still centered on the coffee table and a cottony white cloth with little sparkles had been placed around the base. Maybe at last Reese was starting to find her holiday spirit.

Though the place was clean, it was showing its age. It was very striking how different this apartment was from his polished, well-kept suite. He turned in a circle, taking in the details. The yellowing walls could use a fresh coat of paint. And the ceiling was missing plaster where the roof had leaked.

A thought started to take shape. He might be of royal blood, but that didn't mean he hadn't gotten his hands dirty. Thanks to a very patient maintenance worker who used to be put in charge of him whenever he got in trouble as a youth, he'd learned a lot. Probably a lot more than most people of his status. And it wasn't until now that he realized what a gift it was to have a practical skill set.

He set off to the downstairs in search of Reese. When he couldn't locate her anywhere, he ended up in the kitchen. The chef was there. He was a unique guy, tall and wiry and about Alex's age, maybe a little younger. But his worn face said that there was so much more to his life's story than cooking for pampered guests. Above all that, the guy seemed like an all-around fine fellow.

"Good morning, Bob. Have you seen Reese this morning?"

"Morning. What would you like for breakfast? I can whip you up something in no time. If you want to wait in the dining room, I'll bring it in to you."

"That won't be necessary. I can eat in here." Alex set about getting himself a cup of coffee before Bob could make the offer. "About Reese, have you seen her?"

"She passed through here awhile ago, mumbling something about business to take care of. She wasn't in a talkative mood. Come to think of it, I haven't seen her since. In fact, I'm not used to this place being so utterly quiet."

Bob's last comment stuck with Alex. He never really thought about Reese keeping her staff on duty just for him. That certainly wasn't necessary. He could fend for himself. After all, he was supposed to be just an ordinary citizen—not royalty. He'd have a word with her later.

"Do you like working here?" Alex took his cup of black coffee and sat down at the marble counter.

"I'm lucky to have this job. Reese helped me out at a really bad time in my life." Bob turned back to the stove. "If it wasn't for Reese, who knows where I would have ended up."

"I take it she's a good boss?"

"The best." Bob turned from the omelet he was preparing and pointed his spatula at Alex. "And I won't stand by and let someone hurt her."

Alex held up his palms innocently. "You don't have to worry about me. I'll be moving on soon."

"Good."

"Now that we have that clear, I was wondering if you might help me with a special project."

Bob wiped his hands off on a towel. "Depends on what you have in mind."

"I have some extra time on my hands and I'd like to put it to good use."

"Well, if you're looking for things to do, you can sightsee or hit the clubs. They don't call it the city that never sleeps for no reason."

Alex shook his head. "I had something else in mind. But I'll need your help."

Bob sat an empty bowl in the sink. After a quick glance at the omelet, he stepped up to the counter. "What exactly do you have in mind?"

CHAPTER SEVEN

"WHAT ARE YOU DOING?"

Reese glared up at Alex, who was standing on a ladder in the corner of the living room. With a chisel in one hand and a hammer in the other, he turned. Was that guilt reflected in his blue eyes?

"I got bored." He lowered the hand tools to the top of the ladder.

She crossed her arms. "So you decided to make a mess of my apartment?"

Her gaze swept across the room, taking in the drop cloths covering everything. Cans and tools sat off to the side. And then her gaze settled back on the culprit. Alex was flashing her a guilty grin like some little boy caught with his hand in the cookie jar. But she refused to let his good looks and dopey grin get to her.

"Alex, explain this. What in the world are you doing?"

"Fixing the ceiling."

She frowned at him. What was this man thinking? Obviously he hadn't been when he made
the hole in her ceiling. It would cost a small for-
tune to repair it—money she didn't have. She'd
already made the rounds to the banks. No one
was willing to help her refinance The Willows.
She was officially tapped out.

In fact, she'd returned home determined to figure out a way to meet next month's payroll. She
really didn't want to let Sandy go before Christmas. Reese would do anything to keep that from
happening, but sometimes the best of intentions
just weren't enough.

"Alex, do you know what a mess you've created? There's no way that I'll be able to get someone in here to fix it."

"You don't need to hire anyone. I have this
under control."

Her neck was getting sore staring up at him.
"Would you get down off that ladder so I can talk
to you without straining my neck?"

He did as she asked and approached her. He
was so tall. So muscular. And as her gaze rose up
over his broad chest and shoulders, she realized

having him step off the ladder was a big miscalculation on her part.

His navy T-shirt was stretched across his firm chest. Her mouth grew dry. Did he have to look so good? Specks of crumbled plaster covered him, from his short dark hair to the jeans that hung low on his lean waist. She resisted the urge to brush him off—to see if his muscles were as firm as they appeared.

"If you'd give me a chance, I think you'll be impressed with what I can do."

She didn't doubt that she'd be very impressed, but her mind was no longer on the repairs. Her thoughts had tumbled into a far more dangerous territory.

Her gaze settled on his mouth. Was he an experienced kisser? With his sexy looks, he was definitely experienced in a lot more than kissing. The temperature in the room started to climb. When she realized that he was staring back at her, waiting for a response, she struggled to tamp down her raging hormones.

"You need to stop what you're doing. This—this is a bad idea." She didn't know if the words were meant more for him or for herself.

"Really, I can do this. I used to help—" He glanced down at the carpet. "The guy who fixed up our house when I was a kid. I learned a lot."

She groaned. "When you were a kid? Are you serious?"

"Trust me."

She resisted the urge to roll her eyes and instead glanced back up at the looming hole in her ceiling. A cold draft brushed across her skin. A band of tension tightened across her forehead. She couldn't leave the ceiling in this condition; she'd go broke trying to keep the place warm.

"Seeing as you started this project without my permission, you can't possibly expect me to pay you to do the repairs."

His blue eyes lit up. "I agree. And truthfully, I did try to ask you before starting this, but when you were gone for the day, I thought I'd surprise you."

"Humph…you certainly achieved your goal." She eyed him. "You know I really should toss you to the curb. No one would blame me. Tell me, do you always go around vandalizing people's homes?"

His dark brows drew together. "That's not what

I'm doing. And I've never done this for anyone else."

"What makes me so special?" She stared at him, looking for a sign of pity in his eyes. And if she found it, she didn't care what it cost her. She would show him to the door. She didn't do handouts.

His gaze was steady. "The truth is you'd be helping me."

"Helping you?" That wasn't the answer she'd been expecting. Before she could say more, the phone rang. "Don't move. I'll be right back."

She walked away, still trying to wrap her mind around what had gotten into him. She'd bet ten to one odds he didn't know what he was doing. She really ought to bounce him out on his very cute backside...but she needed the money he'd paid to stay here. Being hard up for money really did limit one's options—she hated learning things the hard way.

Of course when she answered the phone and found an impatient creditor at the other end, it did nothing to improve her mood. The man wanted to know why they hadn't received a payment for the past month. After she tap-danced her way into an extension, she walked back into the apartment. Alex was back up on the ladder, making the hole in her ceiling even bigger. She inwardly groaned.

"Do you ever listen to instructions?" She didn't even bother to mask the frustration in her voice.

He glanced down at her and shot her a sheepish grin. "I want to get as much done today as I can."

"And what if I tell you that I want you to stop?"

His gaze searched hers. "Is that what you really want?"

"It doesn't matter what I want. I don't have the money to hire a contractor. I've got creditors calling and wanting to know why they haven't been paid." She pressed her lips tightly together, realizing she'd spoken those words out loud.

"Are things really that bad?"

She shrugged, not meeting his gaze. "I'll turn things around. One way or the other."

"I'm sure you will." He glanced back at the work waiting for him. "In the meantime, I better get back to work, because I don't want to miss dinner."

She cast a hesitant look back at the hole in the ceiling before turning back to him. "You promise you know what you're doing?"

He smiled and crossed his heart. "I promise."

With effort, she resisted the urge to return the smile. She wanted him to know that she was serious. Was it his sexy accent that made his promise so much easier to swallow? Or was it something more?

"Okay. I have a few things to do before dinner."

She reached the doorway when he said, "You know you don't have to keep Bob around on my account. I can fend for myself."

"This is his job and he's counting on a paycheck. The stubborn man doesn't accept anything that might be construed as charity."

Alex sent her a knowing smile. "Sounds like the pot calling the pot black."

"It's kettle. The pot calling the kettle black."

"So it is. And you, my dear, are the pot."

With a frustrated sigh, she turned her back on Alex and the crater-size hole in the ceiling. She had bigger problems to solve. Like finding a way out of this horrendous financial mess that she'd inherited. The thought of her father and how much trouble he'd brought to her and her mother renewed Reese's determination not to fall for Alex's charm. She needed to keep things simple where men were concerned—especially where Alex was concerned.

Not yet.

Alex groaned and hit the snooze setting on his phone, silencing the loud foghorn sound. He'd been having the most delightful dream and Reese was in it. He'd been holding her close with her generous curves pressing to him. A moan rose in his throat as he desperately tried to recreate the dream.

She'd been gazing up at him with those eyes that could bend him to her will with just a glance. He'd been about to kiss her when the blasted alarm interrupted.

Try as he might, there was no returning to Reese's arms. He rolled over and stretched. Days had turned into two weeks and his body had adjusted to the time change. He wondered how much longer he'd be here.

For the first time, the thought of packing his bags and catching the first flight back to Mirraccino didn't sound appealing. This chance to be a regular citizen instead of a royal prince was far more appealing than he'd imagined— Reese's face and those luscious lips filled his mind.

The images from his dream followed him to the shower—a cold shower. After all, it was only a dream, a really hot dream, but a dream just the same.

He pulled a pair of jeans from the wicker laundry basket. Reese had generously offered to show him how to do his own laundry. He had much to learn, but he didn't mind. However, when he pulled a T-shirt out of the dryer to fold, he frowned. It was pink. Pink?

He balled it up and tossed it aside. His thoughts turned back to his beautiful hostess. Maybe if he were to tell her the truth about himself he could—what? Ask her to hook up with him? No. Reese wasn't the love 'em and leave 'em type.

He pushed the tormenting thoughts to the back of his mind as he finished up his laundry and sat down at his computer. He typed his name in the search engine. In no time at all, there were thousands of results. Good. He had their attention now. His gaze skimmed down over the top headlines: *With Rising Tensions in Mirraccino, Where Is Prince Alexandro? Is Prince Alexandro on a Secret Mission? The Mirraccino Palace Is Mum about Prince Alexandro's Absence.*

The headlines struck a chord with him. He should be at home, helping his papa. Instead he was here, repairing a hole in the ceiling for a woman whose image taunted him at night while her lush lips teased him by day. Still, he was doing an important function. As long as the press was sniffing out stories about him, his family could function under the radar.

A couple of older photos of him popped up on social networks with new tags. They were of him posing with beautiful women. All of them were strangers to him. He honestly couldn't even recall their names. Once the photos were taken, they'd gone their separate ways. *Then he saw one head-line, proclaiming:*

Did the Prince Ditch Duty for Love?

His clenched hand struck the desktop, jarring his computer. No, he didn't. But no one outside of the family would ever know that he was doing his duty—no matter how much it cost him.

No matter how much he hated keeping the truth from Reese.

His gaze roamed over the headlines again and he frowned. No one was going to win his heart. He didn't have time for foolish notions of Cupid and hearts. When it came time for him to marry, it would be because it was what was expected of him.

He wouldn't set himself up for the horrendous pain he'd seen his father live through after his mother's death. Or the years of loneliness. It had almost been too much to observe.

Yet Alex couldn't let the headlines get to him. They created the attention he wanted—even if they poked at some soft spots. He supposed under the circumstances he couldn't be choosy about how the swirl of curiosity happened as long as it worked.

Perhaps it was time to feed the press a few more bread crumbs. He wrote an anonymous email that because of his security precautions would be impossible for the paparazzi to trace.

To whom it concerns:
I have inside information about Prince Alexandro Castanavo's whereabouts. For a little extra money

I have photos. But this information will not come cheap. It'll be worth the hefty price tag. Let's just say the prince is not off doing diplomatic work. Time is ticking. This offer has gone out to numerous outlets. First come, first served.

He smiled as he pressed send. That should spark some interest.

Not about to waste any more time, he set aside his laptop and headed straight to Reese's apartment to check on the primer he'd applied to the walls and ceiling. All the while, his thoughts centered on Reese. He desperately wanted to be up front with her about everything.

But he knew people weren't always what they seemed and that sometimes they were put in positions where they were forced to make choices they might otherwise not make. This financial crisis Reese was facing was one such instance where she might do something desperate to bring in money to keep this place afloat.

And what would be easier than selling the story of a prince undercover while the crown prince eloped with a woman he barely knew? But another voice, a much louder voice inside him, said he was being overly cautious. Reese was trustworthy. And the time had come to be honest with her...about everything.

CHAPTER EIGHT

This was the answer to her problems.

It had to be.

Reese stood in the inn's office, staring at the paintings she'd completed back before she'd dropped out of school. They'd been viewed by notable figures in the art world and generous offers had been made. Of course, in her infinite wisdom, she'd wanted to hold out, so she'd turned down the offers. She'd dreamed of one day having her own gallery showing. Of people requesting her work by name. But all of that had come to a crashing end one snowy night.

Now her only hope to hang on to the only life she'd ever known came down to selling these paintings. And if she didn't sell them, she'd have to let Sandy go just days before Christmas. The thought made her stomach roll.

Who ever said being the boss was a great thing? Sometimes it just downright rotten.

And this was most definitely one of those times.

"What's put that frown on your face?"

She glanced up to find Alex leaning casually against the doorjamb. A black T-shirt stretched across his broad chest. The short sleeves strained around his bulging biceps as he crossed his arms. No one had a right to look that good.

When her gaze lifted to his mouth, he smiled. Her stomach did a somersault. What was it about him that had her thinking she should have taken more time with her makeup or at least flat ironed her hair into submission instead of throwing it haphazardly into a ponytail?

She swallowed hard and hoped her voice sounded nonchalant. "I was thinking."

"Must be something serious."

"I—I just figured out a solution to a problem." She moved away from the canvases, hoping Alex wouldn't be too curious.

"That's great—"

"Did you need something?" She shuffled some papers around on her desk to keep from looking at him. "Please don't tell me there's a problem with the apartment."

"Not like you're imagining. I'm almost finished."

"Really?" This good news was music to her ears.

"Yes. But I wanted to talk to you about something."

"Can it wait?" She sent him a pleading look. "I was on my way out the door."

He didn't say anything at first. "Of course it can wait until later."

"Good." She didn't need any more problems right now. "Do you need anything while I'm out?"

"Actually, I do." He stepped up to her desk. "And your offer keeps me from having to call a cab."

She laughed. "Come on. What was that cabbie's name? Freddy?" Alex nodded and she continued to tease him. "I'm sure Freddy would love to give you a ride."

Alex shook his head vehemently. "That is never going to happen. I think he had delusions of being a grand prix driver."

She patted Alex's arm, noticing the steely strength beneath her fingertips. As the zing of awareness arrowed into her chest, the breath caught in her throat. She raised her head and their gazes caught and held. Was he going to kiss her? They'd been doing this dance for so long now that it had become pure torture. The wondering. The imagining.

Her gaze connected with his. Definite interest reflected in them. Would it be so bad giving in this once and seeing if he could kiss as well as she imagined when she was alone in the dark of the night, tossing and turning?

Alex cleared his throat. "Do you have pen and paper?"

"What?" She blinked.

"I need to write you a list."

"Oh. Right."

Then, realizing she was still touching him, she pulled her hand away, immediately noticing how her fingers cooled off. He was definitely hot and in more than one way. And she'd just made a fool of herself. She'd only imagined he was interested in her. Her cheeks warmed as she handed over a pen and notepad.

His gaze was unwavering as he looked at her. "I appreciate you doing me this favor."

He wrote out the short list before reaching into

his back pocket and pulling out some cash. He handed both over to her.

"I don't need money. After all, it's my ceiling that you're repairing. The least I can do is pay for the supplies."

"And you wouldn't be paying for those supplies right now if it weren't for my idea to surprise you and start the job without your permission."

She had a feeling that the money was being offered because he felt sorry for her. But he made a valid point. With that thought in mind, she folded the money and slipped it in her pocket.

"I should get going. I have to get the truck loaded up." It wasn't until the words were out of her mouth that she realized she'd said too much.

Alex glanced back at the canvases. "Are those what you need put in the truck?"

"Yes. But I've got it."

He strode over to her paintings. "What are you doing with these?"

How much should she tell him? She found herself eager to get his take on her plan. After all, it wasn't as though she could talk to any of the staff. She didn't want to worry them. And her mother, well, even if she was still at the house, she wouldn't understand. She'd beg Reese to keep the paintings—that they were too precious to part with.

But other lives were counting on her now.

Alex stepped over to the cases that held what she thought were her three best pieces of work. "Do you mind if I take a look?"

She did mind, but she found herself saying, "Go ahead. Just be careful. I can't let anything happen to those."

She had to admit that she really was curious about his reaction to her work. Would he like the pieces? Her stomach shivered in anticipation.

Alex took his time looking over each piece. He made some very observant comments that truly impressed her. If she didn't know better, she'd think that he too was an art student.

"Those are very impressive."

"Do you mean it?"

"Of course." He made direct eye contact with her. "You're quite talented."

Sure, she'd been told her work was good by experts, but there was just something about Alex seeing her work that made her feel exposed. Maybe it was that a stranger's opinions could be swept aside, but Alex's impression of her art would stay with her. For a moment, she wondered when his opinion had begun to mean so much to her.

"Do you still paint?"

She shook her head. "I don't have time for things like that these days."

"This place must keep you busy." He glanced back at the paintings. "Are you planning to sell these?"

"I'm going to speak with some gallery owners about showing them. I'm hoping that they'll fetch a good price. A couple of years ago, I had people interested in them. But back then I had bigger plans. I wanted to keep them and have a showing. But life took a sharp turn before any of that could happen...if it ever would have."

"I am sure it would have."

"Are you an artist?"

He shook his head. "I don't have an artistic bone in my body. I can only appreciate others' work. And you're very good."

"Thank you. At one point in my life I thought I'd have a future in art. I'd been dreaming about it since I was a little girl. But things change."

"You shouldn't give up on your dreams. No one should."

She shook her head, wanting to chase away the *what if*s and the *maybe*s. "That part of my life is over."

"You're young. You have lots of choices ahead of you."

"My mother needs me. I won't just abandon her like…erm…it doesn't matter. I don't even know why we're talking about it. I need to get these in the truck and soon I'll have the money to keep the doors to this place open."

What was taking her so long?

Alex paced the length of the living room. She'd been gone all day. How long did it take to talk to a couple of people? Surely they'd worked all of the details of the sale out by now. After all, he hadn't just been boosting her ego—she really was talented.

Now that he'd made up his mind to be honest with her about himself, he was anxious to get it over with. He doubted she would take the news well at first. She might not even believe him. But hopefully he'd be able to smooth things over. He couldn't imagine what it'd be like to have Reese turn her back on him—not speak to him again. His chest tightened. That couldn't happen.

He retrieved his laptop and settled down on an armchair, hoping to find a distraction. He logged on to his computer, anxious to see what the latest gossip consisted of. As long as it was about him and his fictitious romance and not his brother's real-life romantic disaster, he'd be satisfied.

The sound of a door closing caught his attention. He quickly closed his laptop and got to his feet. "Reese, is that you?"

She stepped into the living room. "Yes."

Her tone was flat and her gaze didn't quite reach his. He couldn't help himself—he had to know. "How did your day go?"

Her eyes were bloodshot and her face was pale. "It doesn't matter. I have some paperwork to do. Is there anything I can get for you?"

"Yes, there is." All thoughts of his need to tell her of his background vanished. Comforting her was his only priority. He attempted to reach out to her, to pull her close, but her cold gaze met his—freezing him out. His arms lowered. "You can talk to me. Tell me what happened."

Her eyes blazed with irritation. "Why do you always have to push? Why can't you leave things alone? First it's the Christmas tree. Then it's my apartment. You can't fix everything."

He took a step back, not expecting that outburst. "I am concerned. I'd like to help if I can."

"Well, you can't. This is my problem. I'll deal with it on my own."

No matter how much she wanted him to walk away, he couldn't. The raw pain in her brown eyes ate at him. Reese was the pillar of strength that everyone in this mansion leaned on. It was time that she had someone she could turn to for support.

"You don't have to do this alone."

"Why do you want to get involved?"

"I'd like to think that we're friends and that you can turn to me with your problems."

"You are my guest and I am the manager of this inn. That's all we are to each other." A coldness threaded through her words.

His voice lowered. "You don't believe that."

"I can't do this now." She turned away.

Acting against his better judgment, he reached out, wrapping his fingers around her forearm.

"Don't push me away. Talk to me. Maybe there's something I can do to help."

She turned back, her gaze moving to his fingers. He immediately released her.

She sighed and lifted her chin to him. "I know you're trying to be nice, but don't you understand? You can't help. No one can."

"Something can always be done." He signaled for her to follow him to the couch. "Sit down and tell me what happened. If nothing else, you might feel better after you get it out in the open instead of keeping it bottled up inside."

She glanced around as though looking to see if anyone was close enough to overhear.

"Don't worry, Bob is at the market. And Sandy had to leave early because her little girl got sick and needed to be picked up from day care."

"Oh, no. Is it anything serious?"

"Not from what I could tell. Sandy said the girl hadn't felt well that morning, but she had hoped that whatever it was would pass. Apparently it didn't."

"So we're alone?"

He nodded. "Except for the groundskeeper. But I rarely ever see him inside the mansion. The only time I ever did see him inside was when I first arrived here and he'd dropped by to give your mother a pine cone wreath."

"Yes, Mr. Winston is very good to Mom."

It was good to know that there was someone around watching out for Reese and her mother. But that didn't mean Alex couldn't do his part, too.

"Sounds like Mr. Winston has more than one reason for keeping the grounds looking so nice."

Reese's fine brows drew together, forming a formidable line. And her eyes darkened. What in the world had he said wrong now?

CHAPTER NINE

"THAT'S IMPOSSIBLE."

Reese sat back, stunned by the thought of her mother liking Howard Winston. Her mother was still recovering from the mess after her father's death. Her mother would never let another man into her life, not after the way they'd been betrayed. It wasn't possible. Men weren't to be trusted.

"Are you so sure?" Alex persisted. "I mean, I only saw them together a couple of times, but there was definitely something going on there."

"They're just friends." Reese rushed on, unwilling to give his observation any credence. "Mom would never get involved with another man. Not after…after my father."

She'd almost let it slip that her father was a horrible, lying, conniving man, but she caught herself in time. Airing her family's dirty laundry to a stranger—well, Alex wasn't a stranger any longer. And the truth was she didn't know what he was to her.

Still, she didn't like to talk about her father—with anyone. The man wasn't worth the breath to speak his name. After all, he hadn't even loved them. His own family. He'd scraped off their savings and spent the money on his new woman—the woman he had left her mother for on Christmas Eve. And he'd been such a coward that he'd only left a note. He couldn't face them and admit what he'd done.

The backs of her eyes stung. Why did she still let the memory get her worked up? Two years had passed since her father's betrayal had come to light and her mother had crumbled.

Alex got to his feet. "I didn't mean to upset you. I thought you might be happy about your mother having someone in her life."

"I—I hadn't noticed." She choked the words out around the lump in her throat. "I've had a lot of other things on my mind. This place can take a lot of time and attention."

"Then maybe what you need to do is get out of here."

Her eyes widened. "You mean leave?"

He smiled, hoping to ease the horrified look on her face. "I am not talking about forever. I was thinking more along the lines of an early dinner."

"Oh." Heat flashed in her cheeks. She didn't know why she'd jumped to the wrong conclusion. Then again, maybe she did.

On the ride home, she'd been daydreaming about packing her bags and heading somewhere, anywhere but here. Not that she would ever do it. But sometimes the pressures got to be too much. Just like tomorrow, when she had to tell Sandy that she would have to lay her off. But she would hire Sandy back just as soon as possible—if there was still an inn to employ her.

Alex shifted his weight from one foot to the other. "If you want, we can leave a note for Bob letting him know he can have the evening off."

She shook her head. "I can't afford to splurge."

"Maybe you misunderstood. This is my treat. I think it's time for me to get out of here and check out a bit of New York City. And who better to show me some of the finest cuisine?"

She arched a brow. "Are you serious?"

He nodded.

He was probably right about her getting out of

the house. A little time away and a chance to unwind would have her thinking more clearly. Oh, who was she kidding? There was no way she'd unwind when she knew that she had the horrible task of laying off one of her valued employees, who was more a friend than a worker.

After her father's betrayal, she'd closed herself off, only letting those closest to her in. And the three people who worked for her had gained her trust and friendship. They were a family. They'd filled in when her mother wasn't capable of doing more than caring for herself. They'd been there to support her, to cheer her on, and she couldn't love them more.

Alex shot her a pleading stare. "Surely sharing dinner with me can't be that bad of an idea."

Reese worried her lower lip. She really had no desire to go out, but he was, after all, the paying guest—a guest who'd spent a lot of his time fixing up her private apartment. Giving him a brief tour of Rockefeller Center and dinner was the least she could do.

"I did hear Bob mention that he still needed to run out and buy his girlfriend a Christmas pres ent. I'm sure he wouldn't mind leaving early. I'll give him a call."

"And I'll change out of these work clothes into something presentable."

When he turned away, she noticed how his dark jeans rode low on his trim waist and clung to him in all of the right places. The man was certainly built. She swallowed hard. Any woman would have to be out of her tree to turn his offer down.

She struggled to sound normal. "Um, sure. I'll meet you back here in ten minutes."

He nodded and headed for the steps.

If he was going to dress up, she supposed she should do the same thing. She mentally rummaged through her closet. She didn't own anything special. The best she could do was her little black dress. It was something she kept on hand for hosting weddings.

Some funny feeling inside her told her this dinner was going to be a game changer. They wouldn't be quite the same again. But in the next breath, she assured herself she was making too much of the dinner. After all, what could possibly happen?

* * *

What would it take to make her smile?

Alex sneaked a glance at Reese's drawn white face. The lights of the tall Christmas tree reflected in her eyes, but the excitement that had been there when they'd decorated the tree back at the inn was gone. He had to do something to make things better. But what?

She still hadn't opened up to him. Sure, he'd surmised that her plans to sell her paintings today hadn't worked out, but it went deeper than disappointment. He'd been hoping that when he took her out on the town, she'd loosen up and temporarily forget her problems. So far it wasn't working.

"Maybe stopping here was a bad idea." Alex raked his fingers through his short hair.

"No, it wasn't." She reached out and squeezed his hand. She smiled up at him, but the gesture didn't quite reach her eyes. "It's just that I used to come to Rockefeller Center every Christmas with my father. Back then the tree looked ginormous to me."

"I am sorry that it now makes you sad."

She shook her head. "It's not that. It's just that

back then things weren't so messed up. At least, I don't think they were. I'd like to think that part of my life was genuine and not riddled with lies."

"What lies?" Had he missed something she said? Impossible. He was captivated by her every word.

She shook her head and turned back to the tree. "It's nothing. Just me rambling on about things that aren't important."

He stepped in front of her. "It sure sounded important to me. And I'd like to understand if you'll tell me."

"Why do you care? I am just your host."

"And my friend," he added quickly. Then he stopped himself before he could say more—things that he, the prince of a far-off land, had no right saying to anyone. His feelings were irrelevant. His duty was to the crown of Mirraccino. That was what he'd been telling himself for years.

She smiled up at him. "You're very sweet. It's surprising that you're not taken yet."

He pressed a hand to his chest. "Who would want to kidnap me?"

She laughed. "Your English is very good, but I'm quickly learning that you aren't as familiar with some of our sayings. What I meant was I'm surprised that you're not in a committed relationship."

His thoughts briefly went to the king and his insistence that Alex formalize the plans to announce his engagement to Catherine, an heiress to a shipping empire. The entire reason for the match was political positioning. Combining her family's ships with the ports of Mirraccino would truly make for a powerful resource and secure Mirraccino's economic future. It didn't matter that he and Catherine didn't have feelings for each other. An advantageous marriage was what was expected of him—his wants and desires did not count.

As dedicated as Alex was to the crown, he'd never been able to visualize a future with Catherine. In fact, they planned to get together after Christmas and discuss their options. His gut told him to end things—to let her get on with her life. He didn't like the thought of her waiting around for him to develop feelings for her that obviously weren't going to appear. And marrying her out of pure duty seemed so cold. But it was what his family wanted—what they expected.

Catherine was beautiful and he did enjoy her company, but there just wasn't an attraction. That spark. Nothing close to what he felt around Reese. Now where had that come from? It wasn't as though he was planning to start anything with Reese. The last thing his family needed was another complication.

He didn't want to think about himself. It was Reese who concerned him. "Who put that sadness in your eyes?"

She swiped at her eyes. "It's no one. I—I mean it's the problems with the inn. I just need a quick influx of cash."

"What can I do to make it better?" He would do anything within his power—aside from risking his nation.

A watery smile lit up her face as she shook her head. "You've already done enough."

"But how?" He was once again confused. "You mean my reservation?"

"No, by being a caring friend."

Before he had a chance to digest her words, she was on tiptoes and leaning forward. Her warm lips pressed to his. The breath caught in his lungs. Sure, he'd fantasized about this—heck, he'd dreamed of this—but he never imagined it could be this amazing.

She was about to pull back when he snaked his arms around her waist and pulled her closer. Her hands became pinned against his chest. The problems of the Mirraccino nation and the crown's expectations of him slipped away as the kiss deepened. When she met him lip to lip and tongue to tongue, no other thoughts registered except one—he was the luckiest man alive. Nothing had ever felt this right.

She worked her hands up over his shoulders. Her fingers raked through his hair, causing the low rumble of a moan to form in the back of his throat. Her body snuggled closer but with their bulky winter garb he was barred from enjoying her voluptuous curves pressed to his.

He nibbled on her full bottom lip, reveling in the swift intake of her breath. She wanted him as much as he wanted her. The only problem was they were standing in the middle of Rockefeller Center—and in front of the Christmas tree, no less. Not exactly the place to get carried away.

Still, he couldn't let her go…not quite yet. He'd been with his share of women, but they'd never touched a part of him deep inside. It was more than physical—not that the physical wasn't great. But there was something more about Reese, and in that moment his brain turned to mush and he couldn't put his finger on exactly why she was different.

A bright flash startled him out of the moment. His eyes sprang open and with great regret he pulled away from her. Immediately the cold air settled in, but his blood was too hot for him to be bothered by the crisp air.

"What's the matter?" Reese asked.

"I—I thought I saw something. I am certain it's nothing."

His gaze scanned the area, searching for the person with the camera. Had the paparazzi tracked him down? Had they snapped a picture of him holding Reese close?

He studied the other couples and families with small children. It could have been any of them. He was making too much of the situation. If it was the paparazzi, he couldn't imagine they'd worry about hiding. He was just being paranoid without his security detail.

When he turned his attention back to Reese,

she glanced up at him. Her cheeks had bright pink splotches. He couldn't decide if it was the dipping temperatures or embarrassment. And now that the cold air was filling with white fluffy flakes, his brain was starting to make connections again. He owed her an apology.

Years of being a prince had taught him that there was a time and a place for everything. This was not the time to ravish her luscious lips—he needed to keep things low-key between them. He still had yet to reveal his true identity to her. But he would fix that this evening—no more secrets.

He gave her hand a squeeze. "My apologies. I shouldn't have taken advantage of the moment."

"You didn't." Her gaze lowered. "I'm the one who should be apologizing. I started it."

She had, but he was the one who'd taken it to the next level. When she started walking, he fell in step next to her. Hand in hand, they moved as though they'd been together for years.

She glanced over at him. "Are you still up for going to dinner like we planned?"

"Do you still want to go?"

She nodded.

He was hungry, there was no doubt about that.

But food wasn't what he craved. He swallowed hard, trying to keep his thoughts focused on his mission tonight—being honest with Reese without chasing her away.

Big snowflakes drifted lazily to the ground. They quickly covered her hair, reminding him of a snow angel. He'd never seen anyone so beautiful. It was going to be hard to stay focused on his priorities when all he wanted to do was get closer to Reese. If only his life were different.…

In that moment, he heard the king's clear, distinct voice in his head. *Your life is one of honor—of duty. You must always think of the kingdom first.*

And that's what he was doing, but each day it was getting harder and harder to live by those rules. He glanced at Reese. Definitely much harder than he'd ever imagined.

CHAPTER TEN

REESE WAS SURPRISED by how much she was enjoying the evening. The trendy restaurant had
been mentioned by a few of her guests and she
now understood why. It was cozy with soft light-
ing and a few holiday decorations scattered about.
And the tapas menu was simply divine. She loved
trying a bit of this and a bit of that.

And thanks to the deteriorating weather, the
restaurant was quiet enough to make conversation. Everything was going fine until Alex turned
the conversation back to her. After the waiter delivered the coffee and a slice of triple-chocolate
cake, Alex studied her over the rim of his cup.

He took a sip of the steamy brew before returning it to the saucer. "Tell me about him?"

Reese's heart clenched. "Who?"

Please don't let him be asking about her father.
She never spoke of him…with anyone, including
her mother. And she certainly wasn't about to sit

here in public and reveal how that man had lied to their faces before betraying her and her mother in the worst way.

Alex leaned forward, propping his elbows on the edge of the table. "I want to know about your ex-boyfriend. The man who broke your heart."

She let out a pent-up breath. Josh was someone she could talk about. It'd taken her time to sort through the pain he'd caused, but in the end, she'd realized his lies were what had hurt her the most—not his absence from her life.

"Josh was someone I met in college. He was a smart dresser with expensive tastes. I was surprised when he offered me a ride home from a party one night. When he dropped me off, he was impressed by my family's mansion—if only I'd known then what I know now. Anyway, he insisted I give him my phone number."

Sympathy reflected in Alex's blue gaze. "He was after your money?"

"Yes. But I was too naive to know it then. I let myself get so caught up in the thought of being in love that I let it slide when things always had to be his way. And when he'd criticize my outfits, I thought it was my fault for being so naive about fashion."

"What a jerk." Alex's jaw flexed.

"When my father died, things changed. Josh transformed into the perfect gentleman. He said all of the right things and even talked of us getting married. He made me feel secure."

The memories washed over her, bringing with them the forgotten embarrassment and pain. She blinked repeatedly. She'd been wrong—recalling her past with Josh hurt more than she'd been willing to admit.

Alex reached across the table and squeezed her hand. In his touch she found reassurance and a strength within herself that she hadn't known was there.

She swallowed down the jagged lump in her throat. "Everything was fine until he learned I wasn't an heiress. In fact, I was in debt. Poorer than a church mouse. I don't know if I'll ever get out of debt before I'm a little old lady."

"You're so much better off without him. He isn't worth your tears."

She ran her fingertips over her cheeks, only then realizing that they were damp. "Once Josh knew I couldn't support him, he stopped coming around and didn't return my calls. But by that point, I was so busy looking after my mother and keeping the bank from taking the house that Josh's absence got pushed to the back of my mind."

"I'm so sorry he hurt you like that—"

"Don't be. It's done and over with. I don't want to talk about him anymore." And she couldn't bear to think of that time in her life—it was truly her darkest hour.

"They say talking about things helps you heal."

"I tend to think that chocolate heals all." She took the last bite of chocolate cake and moaned at its rich taste. "Now it's your turn. Tell me more about yourself."

"Me?" His eyes widened. "I'm boring. Surely you want to talk about something more interesting."

She shook her head. "Fair is fair. I told you about my no-good ex. Now it's your turn to tell me something that I don't already know about you."

He leaned back in his chair as though contemplating what to tell her. Then he glanced around.

She followed his gaze, finding the nearby tables empty. Her anticipation grew. He was obviously about to take her into his confidence—what could be so private?

"What if I told you I'm a prince?"

Disappointment popped her excitement. "I'd say you have delusions of grandeur. I thought you were going to be serious."

He leaned forward as though he were going to say more, but her phone chimed. She held up a finger for him to give her a moment as she fished the device out of her purse. "It's my mother. I have to get it."

She got to her feet, grabbed her coat and rushed to the exit, where she'd be able to hear better without the background music. She stepped out into the cold evening air when the chime stopped. Drat. It could be important. She better call back.

The snow was still falling, enveloping everything in a white blanket. Not many people were out in the wintry weather. Those who were had their hoods up and kept their heads low as they moved along the partially cleared sidewalk. Only one man was taking his time and gazing in the various restaurant and store windows. It seemed awfully cold to be strolling around. But to each his own.

The wind kicked up. She turned her back to the biting cold and pulled up the collar on her coat. She'd just retrieved her aunt's number when she heard a man's voice call out. She turned around.

"Hey!" The man who'd been window gazing was now staring at her. "Yeah, you."

Beneath the harsh glare of the street lamps decorated with tinsel, Reese spotted a camera in the man's hands. He lifted the camera and in the next instance a bright flash momentarily blinded her. She blinked repeatedly.

He stepped closer. "What's your name?"

She stepped back. "Excuse me."

Who was this guy? And why had he taken her photo? People on the sidewalk paused and stared at her as though trying to figure out if they should know her. Like a deer in headlights, she froze.

"Come on," the man coaxed. "Give me a pretty smile."

Reese put her hands up to block the man's shot. "I don't know who you are, but leave me alone!"

"How old are you, honey? Twenty? Twenty-two?"

She went to turn back toward the restaurant when she stepped on a patch of ice. Her arms flailed through the snowy air. Her feet slid. Clutching her phone in a death grip as though it could help her, she plunged face-first toward the pavement.

Alex smiled as he traced Reese's steps to the exit.

The evening had gone better than he'd ever imagined. The tip of his tongue traced over his lower lip as he recalled the sweetness of Reese's touch. She sure could turn a kiss into a full-fledged experience. He just hoped that once he convinced her he was telling her the truth she'd understand, because he wasn't ready to let her go—not yet.

He pushed open the glass door when he saw Reese sway and fall to the ground. The sound of her name caught in his throat. He moved into action as a flash lit up the night—the paparazzi.

Right now, his only concern was making sure Reese was okay.

Alex knelt beside her sprawled body. His chest tightened as he waited for her to speak. "Reese, are you okay?"

"I…I don't know. The fall knocked the breath out of me." She turned over on her backside. "My arm hurts, and my knees."

"I'm so sorry." When she started to get up, he pressed a hand to her shoulder. "Sit still for a second and take a couple of breaths."

Alex glanced around, spotting a man with a camera farther down the sidewalk. His gut instinct was to go after the man, but he wouldn't leave Reese. She needed him.

The photographer took a moment to snap another picture before he escaped into the night. Alex was certain that it would end up in the gossip rags that night, but his only concern was Reese.

And this incident was all his fault. He'd gotten caught up in the moment—only thinking of his need to comfort Reese—to be with her. He'd failed to follow any of the safety protocols drilled into him as a kid. He'd gotten so comfortable in his anonymous role that he'd forgotten just how easily things could unravel. Now once again, his rash decision had hurt someone he cared about.

That thought struck him.

He cared about Reese. It was true. But he didn't have time right now to figure out exactly what that meant. Right now he had to determine if she was all right to move. He needed to get them both off this city street. Luckily, with the inclement weather, not that many people were out and about.

"This is my fault." Alex held his hands out to her. "The least I can do is help you up."

"I've got it."

"You need help. You're sitting on a patch of ice." He continued to reach out to her. "Take my hands."

When she went to reach out to him, she gasped.

"What is it?"

"My right arm. I had my phone in my hand and came down on my elbow."

"How about your left arm? Is it all right?"

"I think so."

He gripped her good arm while she held the injured arm to her chest. An urge came over him to scoop her up into his arms and hold her tight, promising that everything would be better, but he knew that could never happen. He'd waited too long. Too much had happened. Things had gotten too out of control.

And now when Reese found out the truth—the whole truth—she'd look at him with an accusing stare. She was hurt because of him. And he couldn't blame her. None of this would have happened if only he had stayed back at the inn. He'd had a plan. A good plan. And he'd abandoned it.

He noticed the grim line of her lips as she cradled the injured arm and he felt lower than a sea urchin. "I am taking you to a hospital."

"I don't need to go. It's just a sprain."

He sent her a disapproving stare. "I insist the doctors have a look at you."

Deciding that her black heels were definitely not to be trusted on the slick sidewalk, he wrapped his arm around her waist. Even though most of the walkway had been cleared, there were still patches of snow and ice. His arm fit nicely around her curves. The heat of her body permeated her clothes and warmed his hand.

At the truck, he paused by the passenger door and opened it for her.

She cast him a hesitant look. "You're going to drive?"

He nodded. "You can't drive with your arm injured. How far to the hospital?"

"It's just a few blocks from here."

"Good." He helped her into the truck and then set out to get her some help.

"I don't understand what that man wanted."

"What did he say to you?"

"He wanted my name and I think my age. If this is some sort of human interest story for the local paper, they have a strange way of conducting themselves."

"Did he mention which paper he works for?"

"I don't even know if he works for a paper. That's just my best guess. When I first spotted him, he was staring in windows. I didn't know what he was up to."

Mentally Alex kicked himself for letting this happen. He was certain that photographer had known who he was and had most likely tracked him from Rockefeller Center to where they'd had dinner. Well, it wouldn't happen again. When he got back to the inn, he would be placing a call to Mirraccino to update the king on the recent turn of events and would request that his security detail be dispatched immediately.

Worry and guilt settled heavily on his shoulders. There was no excuse for his poor behavior. How would he keep Reese from hating him?

In one evening, he'd broken his promise to himself to follow the rules and keep those closest to him safe. He glanced at Reese, who was still holding her arm. He'd failed her in more than one way.

He should have trusted her with the truth about himself before now. But at first he'd worried that she'd sell the information. And then he'd enjoyed his role as plain Alex and selfishly didn't want her treating him differently. Now he'd waited too long.

CHAPTER ELEVEN

WHY WAS HE acting so strangely?

Reese sat on the edge of the emergency-room exam table and studied the drawn lines on Alex's handsome face. She recalled him apologizing and blaming himself for her injury. What was up with that? He hadn't even been outside when she'd slipped.

Why did she have this feeling she was missing something? She was about to ask him when the doctor entered the room.

The gray-haired man in a white coat had a serious expression on his face as he introduced himself and shook her good hand. "The films show you didn't break any bones. However, you have some minor cuts and abrasions. The worst injury is a contusion to your elbow."

Alex's hands clenched as he stood next to her. "How bad is it?"

His worry and anxiety were palpable. Had he

never seen anyone get hurt before? If this was how he reacted to scrapes and bruises, she was really glad there was no blood.

The doctor's brow arched as he took in Alex's presence.

Reese spoke up. "It's okay. He's my friend."

"All in all, she's lucky. We'll clean her up and give her some anti-inflammatories to help with the swelling. She'll be sore for a day or two, but she'll feel better soon."

Reese detected the whoosh of breath from Alex. She'd swear he was more relieved than she was over the diagnosis. Although the thought of a cast was not one she would have relished when she had to take over the maid duties. How exactly would she have changed linens one-handed? Or managed any of the other tasks?

It seemed to take an eternity until she was released from the hospital. She tried to talk to Alex, but his moodiness wasn't of any comfort. When he did speak, it was only in one-syllable answers. You'd think he was the one who'd been hurt, not her.

It was all his fault.

Reese had been put in harm's way. She'd been

hurt. And it was all because he hadn't taken the proper precautions. It wouldn't happen again.

With her snug in bed, Alex moved into action. He had some explaining to do. His papa would not be pleased—not that he could make Alex feel any guiltier than he already did.

While he spoke with the king, Alex scanned the internet trying to locate the photo from this evening, but no matter what he typed in the search engine, nothing popped up. He was certain the man with the camera had been part of the media and not just some fan. So where was the picture?

Alex braced himself for some fictitious story to accompany the photo. He just hoped that it wasn't too scandalous. His family had been through enough with his brother's overnight marriage to a practical stranger.

"You should have listened to me!" The king's voice vibrated the phone. "How badly is the girl injured?"

"She's going to be sore for a while, but there's nothing serious."

"You know that you must make this right. Her injuries are the result of your poor judgment. You shouldn't have been out in public without your security detail."

"I'll do my best to make it up to her."

"Make sure you do. We don't need her turning to the media with a sob story or worse. We're already dealing with enough here."

He would take care of it. But first he had to be honest with her. He just hoped that with her being so loyal to her mother and her need to hang on to this mansion that had been in her family for generations that she'd be able to understand his loyalty to his family and the crown.

"How are things with Demetrius? Have the issues been resolved?"

"Almost. We need another day or two. Can you make that happen considering everything that just occurred?"

"Yes." That was his duty, no matter what.

Alex raked his fingers through his hair and blew out a long slow breath. "I'll make sure our plan does not unravel because of tonight's incident. I already have a backup plan in motion. I will step things up and take care of Reese at the same time."

"I don't like the sound of this. The last time you had an idea, you snuck out of the palace and took too many risks with your safety. This time I insist you tell me about this backup plan."

Alex rolled out his plan for his papa. He also took into consideration the king's suggestions and made a few adjustments until they were both satisfied.

"What about Catherine?"

The muscles in Alex's neck tightened. "I'll speak with her when I get home."

The logical thing would be to go to Catherine and formalize the marriage that their families were so eager to see take place. But how was he supposed to make a commitment to a woman he didn't love?

His priority now was speaking with Reese. He'd do that first thing in the morning. Somehow he had to make her understand his choices were for the best—for all concerned.

She was, after all, understanding and generous with her employees. These were just two of the qualities that he admired about her. He just hoped she'd extend him the same courtesy.

CHAPTER TWELVE

BEEEEP! BEEEEP!

Who in the world had their finger stuck on the front-door buzzer?

Reese groaned. She rolled over and opened one eye. It was still dark out. What in the world? Her hazy gaze settled on the green numbers on the clock. It wasn't even 6 a.m. She still had another half hour to sleep. Maybe they'd go away.

Beep. Beep. Beep.

Another groan formed deep in her dry throat. She wasn't expecting anyone. Maybe one of the employees had forgotten their pass card. Wait. No one came in this early.

Well, she wouldn't know what was going on until she answered the door.

She clambered out of bed and grabbed her old blue robe. Her elbow throbbed. There was no way the wrap on her arm would fit easily through the sleeve. Instead she draped the robe over her shoulder while holding her arm to her chest.

Her bare feet padded quietly across the floor. The door to Alex's suite was just down the hall from hers. There were no sounds or light coming from his rooms. Lucky him. He was probably still enjoying a peaceful night's sleep. Whatever had her out of bed at this hour had better be important.

She glanced through the window that ran down each side of the front door, finding Mr. Winston standing there. What in the world?

"Please come inside." She held the door open for him. "What are you doing here at this hour?"

"I was up early, reading the paper while drinking my coffee, when I stumbled across something you need to see."

"Couldn't this have waited a few more hours?"

"No. In fact, I got here just in time."

"In time for what?" She was thoroughly confused. She really needed a piping-hot cup of coffee to wash away the cobwebs in her mind.

"Read the headline." He held the morning paper out to her. "It'll explain everything."

She accepted the paper and unfolded it. Her

eyes immediately met a black-and-white photo of Alex. Her gaze skimmed the headline: Royal Prince Finds Love.

The breath caught in her throat as she read the words once more. Below the headline was a picture of her on the sidewalk with Alex next to her. Her mouth gaped. The photo had been taken last night.

She struggled to make sense of her rambling thoughts. This is why the man on the sidewalk had been questioning her? Alex was a prince?

How could that be true? Alex was royalty? Impossible.

Then their conversation at the restaurant came rushing back to her. She read the headline again. He had been telling her the truth. Alex was an honest-to-goodness prince.

"It's true," she said in astonishment.

"You know about this?" Mr. Winston's gaze searched her face.

She hadn't meant to say the words aloud. "He mentioned something about this last night."

"Do you understand the trouble we're going to have here?" The groundskeeper wrung his hands together. "I already had to escort two reporters off the property and close the gate. Thank goodness your mother isn't here."

It wasn't just her mother who would not approve of the three-ring circus going on in front of the property. Ever since Reese's father had died, the snooty neighbors had stuck their collective noses up in the air. They didn't approve of the inn. They'd even gone out of their way with the local government and business associations to try to block her from opening The Willows. They didn't want their exclusive neighborhood blemished with a bunch of riffraff.

This latest scandal of sorts would only add fuel to a fire that had finally died down to small smoldering embers. And it was all Alex's fault—correction, it was all Prince Alexandro Castanavo's fault.

She glanced toward the window. "Do we need to call the police?"

Mr. Winston rubbed his gloved hands together. "I don't think it'll be necessary at this point. But if that fella you've got staying here decides to stay on, you might have a real problem on your hands. Do you want me toss him out?"

"Um…no. I'll take care of him." She worried

her bottom lip as she figured out what to do next. "Until he leaves, can you keep the press off the property?"

"I can try. But they could sneak around back without me knowing."

She tapped the folded newspaper against her thigh. "I'll call Bob and ask if he can come help you. Surely they'll get bored and go away soon."

"I wouldn't count on that. They seem to be rapidly growing in numbers."

"Please do your best. And thank you for helping."

Mr. Winston's face softened. "No need to thank me. I'm just glad I was up early and saw the paper."

She marched up the steps, coming to a stop in front of Alex's room. She lifted her hand to knock on his door when her robe slipped from her shoulder. The cool early-morning air sent goose bumps rushing down her skin.

What should she say? Why had he kept his identity a secret? What was he doing here at The Willows? The unending questions whirled round in her mind.

Maybe it'd be best if she got dressed before

confronting him. It'd also give her a moment to figure out exactly what she was going to say to him. Most importantly, she wondered if he was truly going to come clean about last night.

Reese called Bob and then rushed through the shower. The more she thought about how Alex had duped her, the angrier she got. And to think she'd started to trust him—to open up to him.

Minutes later, she returned to his door. With her good hand, she knocked.

There was no answer.

She added more force to her rapid knock. "Alex, I know you're in there. Wake up!"

There was a crash. A curse.

The door swung open. Alex stood there in a pair of boxers. His short hair was scattered in all directions. "What's wrong? Is it your arm?"

"No." She drew her gaze from his bare chest to meet his confused look.

"Reese, what is it?"

"This. This is what's wrong." She pressed the paper to his bare chest. When the backs of her fingers made contact with his heated skin, a tingling sensation shot up her arm and settled in her chest. She immediately pulled away. Now wasn't the time for her hormones to take control. She had to think clearly.

He grabbed the paper and without even unfolding it to read the headline said, "I can explain this."

"So you know what's in it?"

He nodded. "I planned to explain everything in the morning. Speaking of morning, what are you doing up so early? The sun isn't even up yet."

"The sun may not be up, but that didn't stop the reporters from blocking the sidewalk and spilling out into the road. My neighbors are going to have a royal hissy fit over this one."

It wasn't until the words were out of her mouth that she realized her poor choice of words. She looked at him as he moved to the window facing the road and peered out. He was a royal prince. It was taking a bit for her to wrap her mind around that image. To her he was still Alex, who'd stood on the ladder plastering her ceiling. The same Alex who'd kicked back in her living room enjoying a pizza. And the Alex who'd kissed her last night.

She stared at him. His muscled shoulders were pulled back. His tanned back was straight and his head was held tall. And when he turned to her, his faraway gaze said he was deep in thought. His nose was straight and his jawline squared. He definitely looked like a very sexy Prince Charming.

In that moment, it struck her that she was speaking to an honest-to-goodness prince. Royalty. The accusations and heated words knotted up in her throat.

As though he remembered she was still in the room, his gaze met hers. "Do you mind if I throw on some clothes before we get into this?"

Realizing that she was staring at his very bare, very tempting chest, she nodded and turned away. "I'll meet you downstairs."

She headed for the door without waiting for his answer. She needed to talk to him, but not like this. Once he was dressed, she'd be able to have a serious conversation with him.

When she reached the ground floor, she glanced out the front window, finding Mr. Winston strolling along the perimeter of the property. He was such a good guy. She couldn't imagine letting him and the others go. How could she let them down?

She gave herself a mental shake. She would deal with that problem later. Right now she needed to deal with her guest—the man she'd begun to think of as a friend—the man she'd shared a kiss with the night before. She paced the length of the living room. How long did it take to throw on some clothes?

She walked to the foyer and glanced up the staircase. There was no sign of him. With each passing moment, her irritation rose. Why hadn't he been honest with her? Why all of the dodging and evasiveness?

When he finally stepped into the room, she stopped and met his unwavering gaze. His hair was still damp and a bit unruly. He'd put on a blue sweater and jeans. His feet were still bare. She drew her gaze upward, refusing to be swayed by his good looks and his royal breeding. There was something different about him.

"Your hair, it's lighter."

"I started washing out the temporary hair dye."

She openly stared at him. "There's something else."

"I didn't put in the colored contacts."

Instead of a vibrant blue, his eyes were a blue-gray.

"Is there more?" He'd really thought through his charade. Her gaze skimmed over him, looking for any other changes.

"That's all."

She tilted her chin up. "You owe me an explanation. And it better be good. Real good."

"I meant to tell you—"

"When? After you got me under your spell? After we—" She pressed her fingers to her lips.

She hadn't meant to go down that path. In fact, she hadn't meant to mention the kiss, but she just couldn't forget it. Nor could she dismiss the way his touch filled her stomach with a sense of fluttering butterflies.

"It's not what you're thinking. I'm staying at The Willows because I needed someplace quiet to stay."

"Someplace where you could hide from the press?"

He nodded. "This place is private enough while still being close to the city."

"And this explains why you could afford to rent

out the whole place. But why weren't you up front with me?"

"I didn't have a choice—"

"Everyone has a choice. When we started getting closer, I started opening up to you about my past, but you still remained quiet."

"You don't know how many times I wanted to open up to you." He stepped up to her, but she backed away. His gaze pleaded with her. "I really do have a legitimate reason for not telling you the truth. Will you sit down and hear me out?"

She moved to the armchair while he took a seat on the end of the couch. "I'm listening."

Frustration creased Alex's face. "You must believe me when I say the kiss last night was real. And if you deny it, you'll only be lying to yourself."

The memory of his breath tickling her cheek. The gentle scent of his spicy cologne teasing her nose. And then his warm lips had been there, pressing against hers. Alex was right. The kiss had been out of this world.

"You mentioned something about a duty. A duty to do what?" she prompted, trying to keep not only him but also her own thoughts on target.

"To protect my country at all costs."

Reese rubbed the shoulder of her injured arm, trying to ease the dull ache. "Go on."

"I'm sorry about last night with that reporter. You were injured because I didn't follow protocol—again."

"Again?"

He paused as though searching for where to begin. "I was rebellious when I was younger. I hated all of the rules and protocols. I didn't understand their importance. When I was fifteen, I got in an argument with the king before a public outing."

"I'm guessing that was a no-no."

Alex nodded. "I ignored the mandated protocol of staying with the bodyguards at the event and took off into the crowd. With the guards chasing after me, the king and queen were not fully protected. A gunshot by a subversive meant for the king struck—struck my mother."

Reese sat back, stunned by the traumatic event in Alex's childhood. She reached out and squeezed his hand. Sympathy welled up in her for the guilt a fifteen-year-old should never have to experience.

"Before my mother died, she had me make a promise—to take care of Papa. I've kept that promise ever since. It's the very least I could do after what I did."

"Your mother must have loved your father dearly."

"Not always. Theirs was an arranged marriage."

Reese had heard of them existing in some cultures, but she found it startling that people would marry for something other than love. "How did they meet?"

"My grandfather wanted Mirraccino's wine industry to flourish beyond our nation's boundaries. He'd determined the best way to do that was to join forces with one of Italy's major wine producers and distributors. And during one of those meetings, my grandfather was introduced to my mother. It was then and there that my grandfathers came to agreement to merge the families through marriage."

"I can't imagine having to marry someone that you don't love."

"As a royal, one must always do their duty.

It's an expectation that starts at birth." Alex shrugged.

"Lucky for your parents it all worked out—"

"Not quite. If only I'd have followed the rules, she...she might still be here."

"You can't blame yourself. You were young and kids don't think before they act."

"I grew up fast that day. I swore I would toe the line and protect my family at all costs—even at the risk of my own safety. I couldn't bear the thought of losing them both."

"And that's why you kept your identity from me—you were protecting your family?"

"I'm here on a most important mission for my country."

"A mission?" Alarm bells rang in her mind. What sort of situation had he gotten her mixed up in?

"If I tell you, do you promise that it'll go no further than you and me?"

She worried her bottom lip. She wanted to know. She needed to know. But what if it was something bad? She eyed up the man she knew as Alex. Her gut told her that he was a good guy, even if he had misled her.

"It'll stay between us."

The lines in his face eased. "My country is a small group of islands in the Mediterranean. It has a strong hold in the shipping industry and wines."

She listened as Alex revealed some of the history of his islands. She was amazed that his small country could have an uprising. When she thought of a sunny island, she thought of peaceful beaches and lazy afternoons. It just showed that she spent too much time wrapped up in her own little part of the world.

After he explained about his brother's impulsive marriage, Alex looked her directly in the eyes. "So you see how my brother's impulsive behavior would be disastrous for our nation."

She wasn't so sure she saw the situation the same as him. "So what you're saying is that you don't believe in love at first sight?"

He shook his head. "No, I don't. I believe in lust and need. But love…well, it grows over time. Like my parents' marriage."

Reese got his message loud and clear. The kiss last night meant nothing. A pain pinged in her chest. She sucked down the feelings of rejection. After all, it was only a kiss. Right now, she needed to hear the rest of Alex's explanation.

"So you think your brother married this girl just so he could have his way with her?" Reese didn't even know his brother, but she wasn't buying that story.

"I didn't say that."

"Sure you did. But something tells me if he looks anything like you that he could have almost any woman he wanted. So why would he offer marriage if he didn't love her?"

Alex paused and stared off into the distance as though he were truly considering her argument. "Maybe you do have a point. Perhaps he was genuinely infatuated with her."

She laughed in frustration and shook her head. "You just won't give in to the fact that your brother might truly love this woman and that your family is trying to tear them apart."

She was about to ask him what he would do if his family tried to come between them, but she stopped herself in time. After all, there wasn't anything for his family to disrupt.

Alex frowned. "It doesn't matter if he loves her or not. He's the crown prince. A wife will be chosen for him. Just as was done for my father and his father."

She wasn't going to argue his brother's case. It was none of her affair. But the pack of reporters outside was a different matter. "Now that you have the press off of your brother's trail, what are you going to do? The press can't camp out on my sidewalk. The neighbors are probably on the phone with the police right now."

"I have a plan, but I need your help."

The little hairs on the back of her neck lifted. "What do you want me to do?"

He held up the paper. "I need you to play the part of my girlfriend."

CHAPTER THIRTEEN

"I COULDN'T BE more serious."

Alex sent her a pleading look that had a way of melting through her resistance. He wanted her to be his pretend girlfriend? Her, Reese Harding, the girlfriend of an honest-to-goodness prince?

The phone started to ring. This was the perfect excuse for her to escape his intense stare. His eyes on her made her heart race and short-circuited her thoughts.

"You've got the wrong woman." She started for the hallway.

"Reese, please wait. Hear me out." There was a weary tone in his voice that stirred her sympathy.

She stopped but didn't turn around. She knew that if she did she'd cave. And she just wasn't ready to give in to him just yet. "I need to get the phone."

"Let the answering machine pick it up. This is

important." He cleared his throat. "I know I made a mess of this. I'm truly sorry."

She nodded, letting him know that she'd heard him.

"Will you at least look at me?"

Reese drew in a deep breath. Part of her wanted to keep going out the door and let him know that what he'd done couldn't be forgiven with two little words of apology. But another part of her understood where he was coming from. He'd been doing what he thought was right and necessary to protect his family. How could she fault him for that?

"I wouldn't ask you to do this if it were not a matter of national security."

Her gaze narrowed in on him, trying to decide if this was the truth or not. "National security? Shouldn't you be talking to some government agency?"

"Not the United States." He got to his feet and moved to stand in front of her. "My country is in trouble."

That's right. He was a prince. Not Alex the repair guy. Not Alex who helped her decorate the

Christmas tree. And certainly not Alex the laid-back guy who enjoyed an extra-cheese pizza.

"I don't think I can help you. I run an inn. I'm not an actress. I could never pretend to be a rich debutante or some ritzy character."

"But you have something better than money and a well-known name."

"And what's that?"

"You are a woman of mystery. A woman who has the press waiting to eat out of your hand."

She was really getting confused. "What exactly is it you want me to do? Pose for the cameras?"

"In a way, yes."

She shook her head. "I'm not a model. The black dress that I wore last night and ripped on the pavement was my best dress. You'll have to find someone else."

"That isn't possible."

"Sure you can. This is New York City. The place is crawling with single women. And I'm sure a lot would clamor to be seen on your arm."

"But they're not you—the mystery woman in the photo." He glanced away as though he hadn't meant to blurt that part out. "We could make this a full-fledged business deal."

"A business deal?" She pressed her good hand to her hip. "It's really that important?"

He nodded. "If you were to continue our charade, I would pay off the debt on The Willows."

She stared at him. "You can't be serious. Nothing could be that important."

"Trust me. It's of the utmost importance." He leaned back in the ladder-back chair. "When this situation is behind us, you will own The Willows outright. Maybe then you can go back to art school and follow your dreams."

Reese placed a hand on the archway leading to the foyer to steady herself. Had she truly heard him correctly? Impossible. No one could toss around that much money...except maybe a prince. But what struck her even more was the desperation reflected in his eyes. How could she turn him down with so much at stake?

But did he know what he was asking of her? Did he know that her heart was still bruised by the way he took her feelings so lightly? Did he know that kiss was the most amazing thing to happen to her in a very long time?

Pretending to be his girlfriend would only stir up more unwanted emotions. She shouldn't even consider the idea. It spelled trouble with a capital *T.*

"If I agree, how long will this charade go on for?"

"Not long. Once my brother and the king have the situation settled, the press will find another story to interest them. The paparazzi's attention span is quite short."

"So we're talking a few days?"

"Perhaps longer."

"A week? Or two?"

"Maybe longer." When her mouth gaped open, he added, "No more than a month. At most."

Her gut told her to back out of this agreement as fast as possible—to save herself. But another part of her fancied the idea of dating a prince—even if it was all a show. Above all, she wasn't ready to say goodbye to Alex.

Before she could change her mind, she uttered, "Fine. You have yourself a fake girlfriend."

"There's one more thing you should know."

Her stomach tightened into a knot. "There's more?"

"We need to return to Mirraccino first thing in the morning."

"What?" He couldn't possibly be serious. This was just too much. "But I can't leave. It's Christmastime. I—I don't even have any presents bought for anyone."

He sent her a weary smile, as though relieved. "You can buy your gifts in Mirraccino and I'll make sure they're shipped in time for Christmas."

She frowned at him. "You seem to have an answer for everything."

"This is a once-in-a-lifetime proposition. How can you pass it up?" When she didn't say anything, he added, "If I didn't truly need your help, I wouldn't have asked."

"But what about The Willows? I can't just turn my back on it. And thanks to you, the place will most likely be booked solid through the New Year."

He smiled. "See, I told you things would turn around."

"Don't smile. This isn't good. I don't know how to do everything."

"How about your mother? She could run the inn while you're away."

"My mother? I don't think so."

"Why not? She seems fully capable to me. In

fact, she seems to feel a bit left out. She almost glowed when your aunt needed her. Sometimes people need to be needed."

"And you think that she could run this place on her own?" Reese shook her head. "If you'd seen her after my dad died. She was a mess. No, it'd be too much for her."

"I don't think you give her enough credit. Maybe you've been caring for her for so long that you don't even see that she's recovered and ready to take on life if you would just let her."

"And what if something goes wrong and I'm out of the country?"

"Mr. Winston can help her."

Reese's mind replayed how Mr. Winston had always been there, trying to cheer up her mother. And over the past year, he'd made it his mission to bring her a bouquet each day from the flower gardens. She realized that her mother had seemed to spring back to life during that period. Was it possible it had something to do with Mr. Winston?

Her hands balled at her sides as she considered that maybe her mother didn't need her hovering anymore. Maybe it was time her mother stood on her own again.

She tilted her chin up and met Alex's steady gaze. "Tell me what you expect from me in exchange for this all-expenses-paid vacation to some Mediterranean island."

He reached into his pants pocket and pulled out a small black velvet box. "You'll need to wear this."

Reese's heart thumped. She'd always dreamed of the day a man would present her with a diamond ring and ask her to be his wife. What girl didn't at some point in her life? But not like this. She didn't want a fake engagement.

"I can't pretend to be your fiancée."

He gestured to the box in her hand. "Open it before deciding."

She had to admit she was curious to see the contents. The lid creaked open. Inside sat a ring with a large pink teardrop sapphire in the center with diamonds encircling it. The breath caught in Reese's throat. She'd never seen anything so beautiful. Ever.

"Is it real?"

"Most definitely."

"Where did you get it?"

"I had it shipped from Mirraccino. I hope you like it."

At a loss for words, she nodded and continued to stare at the stunning piece of jewelry. She was tempted to slip it on her finger...just to see how it'd look. After all, she'd probably never, ever hold something so precious in her hands again. Talk about your once-in-a-lifetime experiences.

Her gaze lifted to find Alex studying her reaction. She closed the lid and held it out to him. "I can't take this. It's too much. What if I lose it or something?"

"It's perfect for you. And you won't lose it. You're very responsible."

"But people will think that you and I...that we're something we're not."

"That's the point. I need people to talk about us instead of about my family."

As tempted as she was to place the magnificent ring on her finger, she returned the ring box to his hand and wrapped his fingers around it. "We'll be living a lie."

"Why does it have to be a lie? I am giving you this ring. That's a fact. You and I are friends.

That's another fact. What stories people make up beyond that is out of our control."

"Still, it'll be a lie of omission."

"And sometimes a little white lie is more important than the truth. If your friend were to ask you if she looks like she put on weight and she has, would you tell her that she's fat?"

"Of course not." It wasn't until the words were out of her mouth that she realized she'd fallen into his trap.

"I just need a little diversion to keep my family safe and the country at peace. Please help me."

How could she turn away? And it wasn't just about him. It was about the innocent people of his nation, who hadn't signed up for a scandal. Maybe she could help him. Maybe...

"I—I can't give you an answer now." No way was she jumping into this proposition without thinking it through—without the pressure of his pleading stare. "I'll have to think it over and talk to my mother. I'll let you know."

"By tonight."

"What?" He had to be kidding. This was a huge decision for her, to step into the spotlight with a prince and pull off some sort of charade. "I need more time than that. There are things to consider. Arrangements to be made."

"I'm sorry, but this has to happen before someone lets the bat out of the bag—"

"It's cat." When he sent her a puzzled look, she added, "Lets the cat out of the bag."

He sighed. "Someday I'll get all of your sayings straight."

Reese's mind had moved past Alex's loose grasp of idioms. She envisioned escaping the cold and snow to visit a far-off island. And what was even more tempting was being on the arm of the sexiest prince alive.

Some people would think she was crazy to even hesitate. But they hadn't lived the past two years of her life. If they had, they'd be cautious, too.

Still, the thought of jetting off to paradise with Alex made her heart flutter. It'd definitely be the experience of a lifetime. Could she honestly pass up a chance to spend more time with him?

She met his blue eyes. "If I agree to this, and I'm not saying that I will, I'm not lying to people. I won't tell them that you and I...that we're anything more than friends."

"And I wouldn't ask you to."

"Then I'll give you my answer tonight."

She turned and walked away before he could say anything else. She had enough things to consider. She didn't need him adding anything else. Once in the office, she turned off the ringer on the phone. She'd get to the messages shortly. She just needed a moment to breathe.

As she sat there and stared off into space, Alex's words came back to her—he was doing what he must to protect his family and heritage, much like she was trying to protect the patchwork of people whom she now considered her family. They weren't as different as she'd originally thought. The love for those they considered family came first. And this trip would help both of their families.

She really didn't have that much to consider after all. If her mother was able to handle the inn, she would be boarding a plane tomorrow. But when she thought of slipping on that ring and stepping in front of the cameras on Alex's arm, her insides quivered. Thankfully she'd have Alex to lean on. With his dream smile and charming ways, surely he'd be able to distract the paparazzi. He'd have them believing anything he told them.

But what about her? Would she be able to remember that this trip was nothing more than a fantasy and that they were each playing a part? How would she protect her heart from the charming prince?

The big moment had arrived.

A black limousine with diplomatic flags rolled to a stop by the airport entrance.

Alex took a deep breath, wondering if he'd been right to drag Reese into this game with the paparazzi. Still, he couldn't imagine anyone else playing the part of his girlfriend. He had absolutely no desire to hold anyone else's hand or to stare longingly into their eyes—for the media's sake, of course. Oh, who was he trying to bluff? Reese's kisses were as sweet as Mirraccino's juiciest grapes and held a promise of what was to come next.

He glanced over at Reese's now pale face. He hated that their departure had to be made such a public affair. She was wearing the newly repaired little black dress that had done him in the other night when they'd visited Rockefeller Center and he'd at last held her close.

He knew that any attempt to kiss her now would be rebuffed. Reese might have agreed to help him, but things had changed. She even looked at him differently, as though she didn't quite trust him. And he couldn't blame her.

None of this had worked out the way he'd wanted. His gaze slipped to her arm. "How's the arm feeling?"

"What?" She glanced at him with a questioning look.

"The arm—how is it today?"

"Don't start coddling me. My mother did enough of that when she got home yesterday from my aunt's."

He knew to tread lightly around the subject of her mother. Even though all of the staff at The Willows had offered to pitch in extra to help her mother run the place while they were in Mirraccino, Reese was still uncomfortable with the decision. He couldn't tell if it was leaving her mother or if it was letting go of the control she had over the inn, but either way this trip would do her some good. A well-deserved vacation.

"Make sure and tell me if the pain gets worse.

We have some of the finest doctors in Mirraccino. They'll see that you're healing properly."

"Did you see all of those reporters and fans out there? Some are even holding signs."

"Don't worry. We have security. Those people won't be able to get to you."

"Is it always like this when you travel?"

"Not this bad. But I had to swirl up sufficient gossip about my love life to gain the paparazzi's attention." With each passing moment it was getting more difficult to remember what was real and what was fake.

"I'd say it's working." She fidgeted with the hem of her dress. "So do you like all of this fuss?"

"Gaining positive press coverage is part of my duty as prince. A large part of Mirraccino's revenue comes from the tourism industry."

She inhaled a deep breath and lifted her chin to him. "Then let's get this over with."

"But first you will need this." He removed the black velvet box from his pocket and opened it.

She glanced at the ring and then back at his face. There was something in her expression, a tenderness—a question—and in a blink it was gone. Perhaps he'd just imagined it.

She held out her hand for the ring. He could just place it in her palm, but he wanted an excuse to touch her—to recover some of that closeness they'd shared before reality had pulled up the blind on their relationship and left all of the flaws visible under the bright light.

He took her hand in his, noticing how cold her skin was compared to his. Was she truly cold? Or was it a bad case of nerves? Did she also find this moment a little too real?

He slipped the ring on her finger and pushed it over her knuckle. It fit perfectly. And more than that, it looked perfect. He'd picked it out especially for her when this idea had started to take shape. Of course, working with his jeweler back in Mirraccino over the internet had been a bit of a risk, but the ring had turned out better than he'd hoped.

"Perfect."

"What?"

"The ring. It fits perfectly."

She glanced down at her hand, and he wanted to ask what she was thinking, but he refrained. Was she having second thoughts? With them about to face the press, it was best just to let her be. He didn't want to say anything to upset her further.

When she lifted her gaze to meet his, there was such turmoil in her eyes—such agony. His resolve crumbled, spreading like snowflakes in a blizzard. He couldn't just sit by and not at least try to comfort her. He reached out and pulled her close. Her head willingly came to rest on his shoulder. Her silky hair brushed against his neck and the delicate scent of her floral shampoo teased his senses.

"You don't have to worry. I'll protect you." He meant it with every fiber of his being.

She lifted her head and looked at him. "You'll be my Prince Charming and ride to my rescue?"

"Yes." His gaze dipped to her lips. They were full and berry-red. Like a magnet, they drew him in and his head dipped. His mouth brushed her trembling lips.

It took him every bit of willpower to keep from devouring her lips. She tasted sweet and smelled divine. When she didn't back away, he continued his exploration. He'd never known a kiss could be so intoxicating. She tasted sweeter than the finest Mirraccino light pink Zinfandel.

This act of being a devoted couple was becoming more and more desirable with each fleeting second he held her close. He couldn't imagine ever letting her go. He wanted this kiss to go on and on. And if they hadn't been in the back of a hired car with the paparazzi just a few steps away, he'd have liked to find out where this heated moment would lead.

As it was, he was grateful for the tinted windows. There were certain things he must share with the world. This wasn't one of them. This was a very private moment that had nothing to do with providing cover for his family.

His hand slid up her arm and cradled her neck. Her pulse thumped against his palm, causing his heart to beat out a similar staccato pounding. This moment was something he would never forget. Everything about Reese was unforgettable. How in the world was he going to let her walk away when the time came?

A tap on the car door signaled that everyone was in place for them to make their grand entrance into the airport. Reese jerked back, her eyes wide and round.

"It's okay." Alex gave her arm a reassuring

squeeze. "They won't open the door until I signal them."

Her fingers pressed to her now bare lips. They were slightly swollen. And her cheeks had taken on a rosy hue. He smiled, enjoying that he'd been the one to make her look ravished.

"I can't go out there now. I must look a mess."

"You look beautiful."

She reached for her purse. "I need to fix my makeup."

His hand covered hers. "Leave it. You can't improve on perfection."

Her questioning gaze met his and he pulled her hand away from her purse.

"Shall we go?"

"Wait! I—I've never done something like this. What if I make a mistake? What if I say or do the wrong thing?"

"Is that all you are worried about?" His face lifted into a smile. Relief flooded his body.

She nodded and stared at him as though not understanding his reaction.

"You'll do a wonderful job. The paparazzi are already enthralled with you."

"But I don't know how to be a prince's girl-friend."

"You're doing an excellent job." He sent her a certain look, hoping to steady her nerves. "And I don't plan to let you close enough to the press to speak to them. This is more about teasing them and letting them wonder about you and me."

Her shoulders straightened and she blinked away the uncertainty in her eyes. "You really think I can help you do this?"

He nodded. "I wouldn't have asked you other-wise."

She reached for his hand, lacing his fingers with hers.

He gave her a reassuring squeeze. "Ready?"

She nodded.

"Don't forget these." He handed her a pair of dark shades and a big black hat with a wide brim to shield her face from the cameras. "Make the paparazzi work for a close-up of you."

"Part of the cat-and-mouse strategy?"

"Exactly."

She settled the glasses on her face, hiding her expressive eyes. Next he handed over the hat, which she angled off to the side. And last, he helped her turn up the collar of her black wool coat.

"There. All set." Alex signaled the driver.

In seconds, the back car door swung open. For the first time, a natural smile pulled at his lips as he faced the cameras. He was proud to have Reese on his arm.

Alex knew it was dangerous to get too comfortable with this arrangement. Soon the final curtain would fall on their show. The thought niggled at him. Was this all just a show? Or was he more invested in this situation than he was willing to admit?

CHAPTER FOURTEEN

SO THIS WAS PARADISE?

Reese stared out the window as the private jet flew over Mirraccino, headed for the private landing strip used by the royal family. Alex's family. She couldn't believe that they'd gone from a gray, snowy day to clear blue skies. The sandy beaches captured her attention. She tried to restrain her awe over the islands' beauty, but she couldn't help herself. As the plane dipped lower, she had an even better view. Never had she seen such picturesque land—from the tropical gardens to the white beaches.

"This place is amazing."

"I'm glad you think so. Just wait until you see it all up close and personal."

She tore her gaze from the window to look at him as panic set in. "But I forgot my camera. My mother is never going to believe this place."

"I have a camera at the palace you can use." He

leaned back in his seat. "Now you see part of the reason I want to protect it. The subversives have in mind to rip up the protected land surrounding the beaches and turn it all into exclusive resorts and condos. They can't see that they'll be destroying a national treasure."

"And that's what the revolt is over?"

"No. There's much more to it, but it boils down to a very unhappy man who has an ax to grind with my papa about something from their childhood. I have never been privy to the details, as the king says that it is not worth repeating. Either way, I've met the man and he's hard, cold and revels in controversy."

"So if this man learns about your brother's marriage, he'll have more ammunition to use against your family."

"Yes. And over the years he has gained a following of troublemakers who think that they can manage the country better than the king and the governing body. But don't worry yourself about it. You have other things to think about. Like enjoying yourself and smiling—a lot."

She should know more about what was expected of her while she was here. "What exactly will I have to do while I'm here?"

"What would you like to do?"

"I'd like to tour the islands, especially the beaches. They look amazing. Maybe go swimming, except I forgot to pack my swimsuit."

"There's something you should know—"

Her body stiffened. "Not more bad news."

"No, nothing like that. I only wanted to warn you that though it is sunny out, the temperature is cool. So swimming in the sea wouldn't be advisable. However, there's a private pool within the palace walls that you're free to use at your leisure. As for clothes, you don't have to worry. I'll have someone stop by with an assortment for you to choose from."

"But I couldn't. I don't have the money."

"It's a perk of the job. You have to look the part of a prince's...um, girlfriend."

She didn't like the thought of taking handouts. But he was right. Her wardrobe was either supercasual, jeans and T-shirts, or business suits for hosting weddings and events. With her recent lack of a social life, she hadn't needed anything else.

But ever since Alex had dropped into her world, things had changed drastically. In fact, it was just settling into her mind that she would be staying in a palace. An honest-to-goodness palace. This trip had some truly amazing perks—besides the devastatingly handsome guy beside her, who could make her insides melt when his lips pressed to hers.

Her gaze settled on Alex. He leaned back in the leather seat and attached his seat belt as the pilot came over the intercom to instruct them to prepare for landing. This was it. She was about to step into a fairy tale. This would be a story she could tell her children one day—if she ever found that one man she could trust.

Things moved quickly after the plane's wheels touched down. The Mirraccino palace with its enormity and beauty left her speechless, and that didn't happen often. The palace's warm tan, coral and turquoise tones glistened in the sunlight. It reminded her of fine jewelry. Its graceful curves and stunning turrets were regal while reflecting an island flair.

She pointed a finger at the magnificent struc-

ture as she struggled to find her voice. "You…
you live here?"

His eyes lit up and his lips lifted at the corners.
"Yes. I was born here. The whole royal family
lives here. In fact, I need to check in on my papa
and brother as soon as we get inside. I hope you
don't mind."

"Not at all. I know you've been worried about
them. It's really nice how close you are with your
family."

Alex cleared his throat. "We're just your average family."

She couldn't help but laugh. "Not quite."

Nothing about Alex was average. Not the Lear-
jet they flew in on or the magnificent palace he
called home. But there was more than just the
physical elements of Alex's life that stood out.
There was his need to look after her when she
got hurt. And his need to fix her apartment.

But then there was the other side of this man—
the side that withheld the truth about himself.
How did she get past that? And should she even
want to? After all, this whole game of charades
was temporary. She had to be careful not to for-

get that this whole trip was nothing more than to benefit the paparazzi.

A man in a dark suit stepped out of the palace. He didn't smile or give any indication that he even saw her. The man's focus was on Alex. Something told her that he wasn't there to retrieve their luggage—not that she had much. She turned a questioning look to Alex.

His demeanor turned stiff and unreadable. "I need to deal with something. If you want to wait inside, I'll be right in."

"No problem." She didn't have to be asked twice. She was eager to see the interior of this amazing palace.

This all has to be a dream.

Reese resisted the urge to pinch herself.

She entered the grand entryway. Her high heels clicked over the marble floor. She craned her neck, taking in the splendor of the walls and high ceiling. She was in awe of the spaciousness and the sheer elegance of the interior, which included a crystal chandelier. And if that wasn't enough to make a girl swoon, standing before her was a man almost as handsome as Alex—in fact, they looked a lot alike. The man filled out a navy suit with the top two buttons of his blue dress shirt undone.

His hair was a deeper shade than Alex's. But it was the man's eyes that held her attention. They were blue, but there was something more—something she couldn't quite define. Perhaps it was loneliness or pain. Whatever it was her heart went out to him.

He spoke in a foreign language.

She held up her hands to stop him. "I'm sorry. I don't understand what you're trying to say."

"No, it is I who am sorry. I forgot that you're American. Welcome to Mirraccino." His voice was deep like Alex's. "I'm Demetrius. You must be Alexandro's friend."

"Ah, yes, I...I'm Reese." She clutched her purse strap tighter. "Alex is talking with someone outside. He'll be right in."

As if on cue, Alex stepped up behind her and placed his hands possessively on her shoulders, as though they belonged together. "Sorry about that. There's a problem down at the port. But nothing that can't be dealt with later. I see I am too late to make the introductions."

Demetrius stepped forward. "This will give me

a chance to say this once. Thank you both for everything you've done to keep the paparazzi from making this difficult situation even worse."

Reese wasn't sure what to say to the crown prince. Should she just say *you're welcome?* Or offer her condolences on the dissolution of his marriage?

Alex rode to her rescue when he stepped around her. "Is everything resolved?"

Demetrius's shoulders slumped. "She's gone."

"It's for the best." Alex's matter-of-fact voice startled Reese. "You have a duty to Papa. To the nation. That must always come first."

Demetrius's pained stare met his brother's unflinching gaze. How could Alex be so emotionless? Reese obviously didn't know him as well as she'd thought. She struggled to keep the frown of disapproval from her face.

As it was, the room practically vibrated with emotion. With bated breath she waited to see if the brothers would come to blows.

Demetrius's hands clenched at his sides. "That's the difference between us, little brother. I don't believe that duty is the be-all and end-all of life."

"And look what that thinking cost you. You

look terrible and this whole episode was taxing on Papa."

"Just because you can live without love doesn't mean that I can." Demetrius's eyes narrowed. "And don't think I'm the only one who has his future drawn out for them. You have no more freedom than I do. And we all know that you're the good son who'll marry whoever they choose for you—"

"Enough." Alex's voice held a hard edge. "I know this is a hard time for you, but we have a guest."

Demetrius's gaze moved to Reese. "I'm sorry you had to witness that. Just be glad that you're here doing a job and you didn't actually fall for my brother. He can be heartless at times."

Before she could even think of a response, Demetrius stormed out of the room.

She turned a startled look at Alex. "How could you say that to him? Couldn't you see the pain he's in?"

"He has to remember what's at stake. Living here—" he waved his hands around "—comes with responsibilities others don't think of. My brother can't afford to forget that his decisions affect far more than just himself. He'll get over that woman."

Reese's mouth gaped open. "I was wrong. I'm not the grinch around here. You are."

"What's that supposed to mean?"

"Read the book, you'll find out. And maybe you'll learn a lesson, too."

His forehead wrinkled. "I don't need a child's book to tell me that there's no room for romance when it comes to the future of this nation."

"And you had to remind your brother of that right now when you can plainly see that he's brokenhearted?"

Alex raked his fingers through his hair. "You're right. I didn't handle it very well."

"That's an understatement." There was one more thing that she had to know. "Is he right? Will a wife be chosen for you?"

Alex's gaze met hers. "My family has plans for me to make an advantageous marriage to a woman from an influential family. We are a small nation and in these uncertain times we can't have enough allies."

Reese's heart sank. "Will you go through with it? Will you marry who they choose?"

He sighed and raked his fingers through his dark hair, scattering the strands. "I don't know. I have more to consider than my happiness. If my marriage can benefit Mirraccino, I must take that into consideration."

All of a sudden this scenario was beginning to sound all too familiar. What was it about men putting everything ahead of love? Did they really think you could sustain a meaningful relationship without it?

She glared at Alex, letting her anger mask her disappointment. "You're just like Josh—"

"What?" Hurt reflected in Alex's eyes. In a blink it was replaced with a hard wall that locked her out. "I can't believe you'd compare me to him."

"Both of you are out to have relationships with women you think can help you. It doesn't matter if you care about them or not. All that matters is what you can get from them."

"That's not true. I'd never lead a woman on."

"True." He definitely wouldn't do that. "You'd tell them up front what you wanted."

Alex reached out to her, but she backed away. "You're tired after our long trip and you're letting my brother get you worked up. We can talk about this later."

He was right. She was getting worked up. But she refused to let another man hurt her—betray her. And the thought of Alex belonging to another woman hurt more than she wanted to admit— even to herself.

"Go after your brother and make things right."

Alex's eyes widened as though he wasn't used to being ordered around. "You're serious?"

"Yes. Go."

"I'll send someone to show you to your room. Later, I'll give you the grand tour."

She nodded her approval. "I need to call my mother and check on things."

Armed with the knowledge that Alex would have a bride chosen for him, she'd have to be careful going forward. She didn't want to get swept up in paradise with a sexy prince and lose her heart. Because in the end, she'd be going back to New York.

Alone.

CHAPTER FIFTEEN

IT WAS JUST the two of them, at last.

Alex stopped next to Reese in front of the glass doors leading to the garden. He hoped a good night's sleep had put her in a better frame of mind. She had to be overcome with exhaustion to accuse him of being anything like her ex-boyfriend. He was nothing like that jerk. He'd never intentionally use a woman. She just didn't understand how things worked when you were born into royalty.

"How are things between you and your brother?" Reese asked, drawing him from his thoughts.

"Getting better. You were right. He really cared about that woman."

They stepped onto the patio and Reese glanced up at him with those big brown eyes. "Does this mean you now believe in love at first sight?"

Alex smiled, amazed by her persistence. "I'll

take it under advisement. Perhaps there's more to this love thing than I understand."

She smiled, too, and he had to resist the urge to plant a kiss on her upturned lips. He didn't want to press his luck. At least today she was speaking to him and not glaring at him as though he was the enemy.

They descended the sweeping steps to the edge of the sculpted garden. The sun was high overhead. He enjoyed the fact that she had on a teal dress that he'd personally picked out. When he'd first laid his eyes on it, he'd known it would look spectacular with Reese's long auburn hair.

"You look beautiful."

"Thank you. I don't even want to think how much this dress must have cost you. Did you know that it has a designer label?"

He smiled, enjoying the enthusiasm in her voice. "All that matters is that you like it and you look beautiful in it."

She ducked her head. "I considered not wearing it. It has to be so expensive. I didn't want to do anything to ruin it. But then I realized that I don't own anything suitable to wear here. And I didn't want to embarrass you."

"You could never do that." And he meant every word. He was proud to be seen with a woman who was just as beautiful on the inside as out.

She stopped in front of him and turned. Her shoulders straightened and her chin tilted up. "Tell me about her."

"Who?"

"The woman your family wants you to marry."

He resisted the urge to roll his eyes. "You don't want to hear about Catherine."

"Catherine. That's her name?"

"Yes." He didn't like where this conversation was headed. "There are some flowers over here that I think you'll like."

Reese didn't move. "This Catherine. What does she think of you being in the papers with me?"

"I—I don't know." He hadn't thought about it. Perhaps he should have let her in on the plan, but they'd never made a point of being a part of each other's lives. "We don't talk very often."

"But you're supposed to marry her."

"It's what our families have arranged. It's what is expected of us."

"But neither of you has agreed to the arrangement?"

Was that a glimmer of hope in Reese's eyes? Was she hoping there was room in his life for her?

"Catherine and I have never talked about marriage. We're friends and we spend time together when our families visit."

"Do you love her?"

At last, the question he'd been certain would come up. "Catherine is a wonderful friend. And a very sweet person. But no, I'm not in love with her."

Reese's mouth settled into a firm line as she glanced away, leaving him to wonder about the direction of her thoughts. He'd rather she get it all out in the open, but instead of prodding her, he remained silent. She was at least still here with him. He shouldn't push his luck.

Reese set off down one of the many meandering paths in the sprawling garden. It amazed him how fast she could move while wearing those silver high heels—but boy, was it a sight worth beholding. As she turned a corner, he realized she was getting away. He set off after her.

He'd just caught up to her when she came to an abrupt halt. It was all he could do to keep from running into her. His hands came to rest on her shoulders as he regained his balance. He was just about to ask what she thought she was doing when his gaze settled on the king.

His papa had stopped in front of them. "I didn't know anyone ever took the time to stroll through the gardens."

Alex glanced at Reese's wide-eyed stare and immediately knew that she was intimidated by not only his papa's title but also his booming voice. "I was just showing Reese around."

"There's lots to see. Your mama firmly believed that it was necessary to pause every day and smell the roses. Your mama knew what was important in life. Sometimes I wonder if she'd approve of my choices, especially with you boys."

Alex was rendered silent, unused to seeing his papa in this state of contemplation concerning his family.

Reese cleared her throat. "I think you've done a great job with Alex. He's kind and thoughtful. You should be proud of him."

"I am." The king's tired face lit up. For a moment, he studied Reese. "Perhaps I am worried for no reason. Now, make sure my son shows you the yellow roses. They were his mama's favorites. If you'll excuse me, I've got to get back to work."

As his papa walked away, Alex was struck by how much his papa still vividly loved his mama. Alex wondered what it must be like to experience such a profound love. But was it worth the risk of ending up alone like his papa—

"Did you hear me?" Reese sent him a puzzled look.

"I'm sorry. What were you saying?"

"I wanted to know which direction led to the roses."

He led her along the wide meandering path edged with low-cut hedges that formed various geometric planting spaces. Each section was planted with just one type of flower, fruit or vegetable. Even though he'd lived here his whole life, he still found the vibrant colors beautiful, but today he only had eyes for Reese.

"With all of these gorgeous flowers, it's like paradise here. You're so lucky."

He looked around the vast garden. He definitely saw it in a different light after living in

Reese's world for a few weeks. And though he was blessed financially, Reese was much better off. Her life contained priceless things such as the wonderful relationship she had with her mother, who obviously loved her very much. And even the people who worked for Reese were totally devoted to her.

His guards were devoted to him to the point of laying down their lives to protect him, but it wasn't out of love. It was a duty—an allegiance to a greater good. He wondered what it would be like to have a warm relationship with those around him like Reese had with her staff.

She glanced at him. "You seem to have a lot on your mind."

"I was thinking that until now I've never considered myself lucky. Sure, I appreciate the fact that I lead a privileged life, but sometimes I wake up and wish I had a normal life."

"You can't be serious. You'd really want to give all of this up?"

He shrugged. "Sometimes. When the rules and duties dictate my entire life."

Her forehead wrinkled. "You mean like now,

when you had to drop everything and fly to New York?"

"Actually, that's something I'll always be grateful for." He stopped walking and turned to her. "It gave me the opportunity to meet you."

"Are you flirting with me?"

"I don't know. Is it working?"

A hint of a smile pulled at her rosy lips. "What do you think?"

His heart thumped against his ribs. The sun glistened off her auburn hair and her eyes sparkled. He was drawn to her as he was drawn to none other. His fingers stroked her cheek and she leaned ever so slightly into his touch.

His royal duties and the knowledge that Reese would never fit into the king's idea of the proper wife fled his mind. In this moment, the only thing that mattered was the woman standing before him with longing in her eyes—such beautiful eyes.

His head dipped down and her soft lips were there meeting his. He moved slowly at first. Like a bird to nectar, he didn't want to startle her. But when she matched him move for move, his heart pounded harder. Faster.

An overwhelming need grew in him for more of this—more of Reese. His arms encircled her waist, pulling her flush to him. He'd never experienced a kiss so tantalizing, so sweet. And he'd never wanted someone so much in his life. Not just physically. Her very presence in his life was like a smoothing balm, easing away the rough edges. It was as if he'd donned a pair of glasses and could see things so much more clearly.

A gentle moan swelled in his throat as her fingers threaded through his hair. He wanted more, oh, so much more. He needed to move them out of the garden. Someplace where they wouldn't be under constant supervision of the security detail—someplace where they could see where this would lead.

There was the sound of hurried footsteps followed by someone loudly clearing his throat. Alex knew the sound—it was time to get back to work. Damn. Why did duty call at the least inopportune times?

With great reluctance he released Reese. "I must go. I've been waiting on an important call."

It was as though he could see the walls rising between them in Reese's eyes. He couldn't blame her for wanting to come first in someone's life. The men in her life had relegated her to an afterthought and collateral damage. She deserved so much better. Not that he was the man to give her all the love she deserved.

As he walked away, he inwardly groaned. His common sense and emotions warred with each other. When it came to Reese, she had him reconsidering everything in his life.

Reese was in dangerous territory.

And though she knew that Alex could never have a future with her, she couldn't resist his sultry kisses. Or keep her heart from pounding when his fingers touched hers.

She needed some space—a chance to clear her mind and remember that this was just a show for the press. But there was no time for getting away. There was no chance for her to be alone except at night in her room. They had a job to do—keep the press concentrating on them while his brother pulled himself together and the last of the legal negotiations were handled.

And this morning, Reese and Prince Alexandro were about to have their first press-covered outing. Alex's long, lean fingers threaded through hers as they strolled along the palace drive on their way to tour the nearby village of Portolina. His grip was strong and she drew comfort from it as she was about to be paraded before the cameras.

This public appearance didn't require big sunglasses or hats to hide behind. Instead Reese had selected a pair of dark jeans, a navy blazer and a white blouse. Alex had advised she dress casually. She hoped her choice in clothes would suffice.

Reese gripped Alex's hand tighter. When he glanced her way, her stomach quivered. But it had nothing to do with the reporters waiting for them on the other side of the palace gates. No, the fluttering feeling had everything to do with the man who had her mind utterly confused between her want to continue the kiss from yesterday and her need to protect herself from being hurt when this fairy tale ended.

Alex leaned over and whispered in her ear, "Trust me. You'll be fine."

She let out a pent-up breath and nodded. They approached the gate as it swung wide open. She faced the paparazzi's flashing cameras and smiled brightly.

"When will the formal engagement announcement be released?" shouted a reporter.

"Is there a ball planned to celebrate the impending nuptials?"

"When's the wedding?" chorused a number of voices.

"The palace has no comment." A spokesman stepped forward as planned to field the questions. "Prince Alexandro and Ms. Harding are out for a stroll about the village. If there are any announcements to be made in the future, my office will notify you."

Security cleared the drive for them. Reese wasn't sure her legs would support her—her knees felt like gelatin. As though Alex understood, he moved her hand to the crook of his arm for additional support and then covered it with his other hand.

As they made their way toward the small village, he leaned over and whispered in her ear, "You're doing great. Now they'll never guess your deep dark secret."

She turned to him and arched a questioning brow.

He leaned in again. His minty-fresh breath tickled her neck, sending delicious sensations racing to her core. His voice was low but clear. "That you're a bit grinchy. And that beneath that makeup you're really green."

She laughed and the tension in her body eased. "You looked up the story I told you about."

He nodded and returned her smile. So he really did hear what she said. Her lips parted as her smile intensified.

With the paparazzi trailing behind, Alex gave her a walking tour of Portolina—a small village near the palace. If not for the festive red-and-green decorations, it would not seem like Christmas—at least not the cold, snowy Christmas that Reese was accustomed to in New York.

The stroke of Alex's thumb against the back of her hand sent her pulse racing as she tried to keep her attention focused on this fascinating town. It was teeming with history, from the old structures with their stone-and-mortar walls to the stone walkways. She even found the doorways fascinating, as some were rectangular and others were arched. Beautiful old brass knockers adorned the heavy wood doors. This place definitely had a unique old-world feel to it. She could see why Alex and his family weren't eager to bulldoze this place and modernize it with condos.

Some people rode scooters but most villagers walked. Many of them smiled and waved. Some even came up to Alex—their prince—and greeted him like some returning hero. But most of all, she could feel their gazes on her. Of course, Reese couldn't tell if they were curious about her or the caravan of reporters. She noticed how Alex barely gave the paparazzi much notice. He merely went about his day and she tried following his lead, enjoying the sights and sounds.

The paths he led her on ebbed and flowed through the village, sometimes between buildings and sometimes under passageways. It was so different from her life in New York City. With the camera Alex had lent her, she took dozens of photos—eager to remember every moment of this amazing trip.

They sat down in a coffeehouse that had been closed to the public. Alex lifted her hand and kissed it. "What's bothering you, *bella?*"

Her heart stuttered as she stopped and stared at him. His reference to her with such an endearing term caught her off guard. But before she let herself get caught up in the moment, she reminded herself that this was all an illusion. She pulled her hand away. He was playing his part—acting like the ardent lover. Nothing more.

But if that was the case, why was he doing it when there was no one within hearing distance? Reese could feel her last bit of resolve giving way. And as he once again reached across the café table to her, she didn't shy away. His warm hand engulfed hers reassuringly. She could feel her resistance to his charms crumble even further.

"You can tell me anything." His voice was soft and encouraging.

Glancing around just to make sure they were in fact alone, she lowered her voice and said, "They expect us to get married. This is what I was worried about. They've jumped to the wrong conclusion. I'll have to call my mother and warn her not to believe anything she reads in the paper."

Reese glanced down at the ring causing all of the ruckus. She wiggled her finger, enjoying the way the light danced over the jewels. It truly was the most beautiful ring she'd ever seen.

Alex waved away her worries. "Don't worry about it. Just enjoy yourself." There was a pause and then he added, "You are enjoying yourself, aren't you?"

"Yes. But when this illusion ends, everyone will think it's my fault."

"*Bella,* you worry too much. After all, you are forgetting that I control what information is fed to the press. On my honor, I promise your good name will remain intact."

She wanted to smile and take comfort in his words, but she couldn't. They weren't the words she was longing to hear. She wanted him to say that she mattered to him. That this illusion was real to him. That it wasn't going to end.

After their extensive lunch was served, the waiter brought them espresso to wash it down. Reese, not used to such a large meal, wasn't sure she had room for it.

Alex took a sip of the steaming brew. "I have some meetings this afternoon that I must attend, but feel free to finish touring the village."

"I think I'll do that. I still have my Christmas shopping to do."

"I promise to return as soon as I can."

"Don't rush on my account. I know that you have important issues to attend to."

"Nothing is more important than you." His warm gaze met hers and her insides melted. "You're my guest and I want you to be happy here. I hope the paparazzi's attention has not been too much for you."

"Actually, your staff has done a great job of keeping them at a distance. And I think the people of Portolina are amazingly kind. You're lucky to live here. I'll never forget my visit."

Her heart pinched at the thought of one day waking up and no longer bumping into Alex. She didn't know how someone she'd only met recently could become such an important part of her life.

She brought her thoughts up short. This was ridiculous. She was falling for her own PR scam. They weren't a couple. And he wasn't someone that she should trust, but with each passing day she was finding her mistrust of him sliding away.

Maybe like the Grinch, Alex's heart was starting to grow. Which gave her a great idea for a Christmas present. There was a small bookstore just back a little ways. She would get him a copy of *How the Grinch Stole Christmas*. Perhaps it wasn't too late for him to see life differently.

CHAPTER SIXTEEN

How could it be more than a week since they'd arrived in Mirraccino?

Alex's body tensed as he realized there was no longer a need for Reese to stay—except for the fact that he wasn't ready to let her go yet. He'd spent every available moment with her, and he still hadn't gotten his fill of her. He'd never had this sort of experience with anyone before.

They'd toured Mirraccino's finest vineyards and taken a trip to the bustling port on the other side of the island. The outings allowed her to rest her arm and the bruises time to begin to fade. And best of all, her frosty demeanor had melted beneath the bright sunshine.

He knew as Prince Alexandro, he should end things here and now. But the plain, ordinary Alex didn't want to let go. He couldn't imagine Reese being gone from his life. How did one return to a dull and repetitive life after being shown a bright, sparkling world full of hope?

Alex had made his decision. No matter what the king said, it was simply too soon for Reese to leave. His brother, the crown prince, was simply not in good enough spirits yet to deal with the press. It wouldn't take much for them to notice the crown prince's melancholy expression. He wore it like an old war wound, reminding his whole family of what he'd lost in order to uphold his royal duty.

Thanks to Reese, Alex was starting to believe his brother's feelings for the woman had run much deeper than he'd originally thought. The price of being royal could cut quite deep at times. He was about to pay his own dues when Reese left for the States. He wasn't relishing that impending day. In fact, he refused to think of it today.

Christmas Day had at last arrived and the paparazzi had fled for their own homes, leaving everyone at the palace in peace—at least for one day. And now that the official photos had been taken, the gifts opened and the extravagant lunch served, he had a very special surprise in mind for Reese. He'd been working on it all week and now he was anxious to surprise her.

"I can't believe the size of your Christmas tree." Reese's voice was full of awe as they strolled back to their rooms, which were in two different wings. "It's a good thing I remembered to have you take my picture next to it. My mother never would have believed it was, what—twenty feet tall?"

"I don't know." He smiled over the things that impressed her. "If you want I can inquire."

"No. That's okay. The picture will say it all. You did get the whole tree in the picture, didn't you?"

"Yes. Now I have a question for you." He sensed her expectant look. "After we change clothes, would you join me for a stroll along the beach?"

"I don't know." Her gaze didn't meet his. "I'm kind of tired. It's been a really long day."

He wasn't going to give up that easily. This was far too important—he had a very special surprise for her. "Or is it that you stayed awake all night waiting for Santa?"

There was no hint of a smile on her face. "Something like that."

"I was only teasing you."

"I know." She continued staring at the floor.

His finger lifted her chin. Sadness reflected in her eyes. "Reese, talk to me. I'll make it better."

She shook her head. "You can't. No one can."

His voice softened. "Sometimes talking things over can make a person feel better."

She leaned her back against the closed door and pulled at the short sleeves of her midnight-blue dress. "Do you really care?"

His fingers moved some loose strands of silky hair from her face and tucked them behind her ear. "You know I do. I care very much."

Reese glanced up and down the hall as though to confirm that they truly were alone. This must be more serious than he'd originally thought.

"Why don't we step into your room?" he suggested.

She nodded and turned to open the door. Inside, she approached the bed, where she perched on the edge. With the door closed, no one would bother them. Alex's mind spiraled with all of the intimate possibilities awaiting them. Perhaps this hadn't been such a good idea for a serious talk.

Reese lifted her face. Her shiny eyes and pale

face stopped his wayward thoughts in their tracks. He sat down beside her and took her hand in his.

Her voice came out very soft. "I was up last night thinking about how my life has changed since my father died at Christmas two years ago."

The news smacked into Alex, stunning him for a moment. "I had no idea."

"I didn't want to make a big deal of it. It was Christmas Eve, to be exact. He was leaving… leaving me and my mother to meet his longtime lover." She swiped at her eyes. "He didn't even have the nerve to tell us to our faces. He wrote a note. A note! Who writes a note to tell the people that he is supposed to love that their lives were a lie and he doesn't love them and he wants out?"

Alex didn't have a clue what to say. Her rigid back and level shoulders sent keep-away vibes. So he sat there quietly waiting for her to get it all out.

"He hit a patch of black ice and went over an embankment. They say he died on impact. He didn't even have the decency to stick around to say goodbye. There was no time for questions—

and no answer to why he'd destroyed our family. It was all over in a heartbeat."

"I'm so sorry he did that to you and your mother."

Reese swiped at her eyes. "At the time, I thought I had Josh to lean on. He was there for the funeral. He was the perfect gentleman, sympathizing with me and my mother." A hollow laugh echoed from her chest. "He had the nerve to condemn my father for his actions. And yet when it came to light that the savings had been drained off and the mansion had been mortgaged to pay for my father's new life, Josh couldn't get out the door fast enough."

Her shoulders drooped as she got the last of the sad story out. It was as though without all of the anger and pain, she deflated.

Instead of words, he turned, drawing her into his arms. She didn't resist. In fact, she leaned into his embrace. Maybe his plan for today wasn't such a good idea after all.

Reese inhaled a shaky breath. "Now you know why I've been so hesitant to trust you—to trust anyone."

Alex lifted her chin with his thumb. When her

brown gaze met his, he said, "You can trust me. I promise I won't abandon you and I won't betray you."

He leaned forward, pressing his lips gently against hers in a reassuring kiss. Her bottom lip trembled beneath his. He didn't know how anyone could take her for granted. Reese was everything he'd ever wanted in a woman and more.

She pulled back and gave him a watery smile. "Thank you. I didn't mean to put a damper on the day."

"And if I had known what a tough day this would be for you, I wouldn't have tried to talk you into an outing."

"The truth is, I'll never be able to relax now."

"Are you saying you want to go?" He didn't want her to do anything that she wasn't up for.

She nodded and wiped away the moisture on her cheeks. "Just let me get changed."

"I'll meet you back here in ten minutes."

"Sounds good. Thank you for listening and understanding." The smile that touched her lips this time was genuine, and it warmed a spot in his chest.

On second thought, maybe his plan was just

what she needed to push away her not-so-happy past and replace it with new, happy memories. Yes, he liked that idea. Reese deserved to be happy after the way she went out of her way for the people in her life—he wanted to be the one who went out of his way for her.

In that moment, he realized something that he'd been avoiding for a while now. He had feelings for Reese—deep feelings. He knew it was a big risk with his heart. Thoughts of his heartbroken father flashed through his mind. But in the next breath, he envisioned Reese's face.

He didn't have a choice.

Somehow, someway, she'd sneaked past his defenses. He cared for her more than anyone else in his life. But he didn't know what to do with these feelings. He was a prince. There were expectations he must fulfill for the good of the kingdom.

As he headed for his suite, he realized it was time he called Catherine. They needed to meet after the holidays were over. In light of his genuine feelings for Reese, he couldn't let the lingering questions surrounding the anticipated royal engagement drag on.

Although with all that hinged on the engagement, breaking the news to Catherine would have to be handled face-to-face and very carefully.

Reese's mouth gaped.

Gripping the red beach bag hanging over her shoulder and with Alex holding her other hand, she stood on the sand utterly speechless. Her gaze searched his smiling face before she turned back to the towering palm tree all decked out with white twinkle lights. The scene belonged on a postcard. It was picture-perfect...just like Alex in his khaki pants and white shirt with the sleeves rolled up and the collar unbuttoned.

Alex gave her hand a squeeze. "Do you like your surprise?"

"I love it." She nodded and smiled. Her gaze roamed around, trying to take it all in. "Is this all for me?"

His eyes lit up as he gazed at her. "It's my Christmas present to you."

The wall around her heart that had been eroding all week completely crumbled in that moment. She was totally vulnerable to him and she didn't care. "But you've already given me so much that I can never repay."

"That was all about our deal. This, well, this is because I wanted to do something special for you." He shifted his weight from one foot to the other. "And I know how much you enjoy the little lights, so I ordered enough to decorate the bungalow inside and out. Do you like it?"

She nodded vigorously. "No one has ever done anything so thoughtful for me. Thank you."

She lifted up on her tiptoes and without thinking of how their diverse lives would never mesh, leaned into him and pressed her lips to his. She heard the swift intake of his breath. They'd been building toward this moment since their first kiss at Rockefeller Center. With each touch, look, kiss, she felt a heady need growing within her. The electricity between them had crackled and arced ever since they met. And now beneath the darkening Mediterranean sky, it had the strength of a lightning bolt. Her insides warmed with undeniable anticipation.

She swallowed hard, trying to regain her composure. "Are you going to show me the inside?"

He blinked as though he, too, had been thoroughly distracted by the kiss that promised more to follow. "Um…yes. Lead the way."

She easily made it up the stone steps that meandered up the embankment and led to a wide-open terrace with a white table and matching chairs. An arrangement of red poinsettias was placed in the center of the table, where a burning white candle flickered within a hurricane lamp. She wondered if his attention to details extended to all parts of his life.

She stopped on the terrace and turned to Alex. This night was so romantic, so perfect. Her heart thumped against her ribs. He'd done all of this for her. With every passing moment it was becoming increasingly difficult to remember that she was only playing a part for the sake of his nation's national security.

And then her chest tightened. Her palms grew damp. And she bit down on her lower lip. In that moment, she remembered how much it hurt when happy illusions shattered and reality ran up and smacked her in the face. She'd promised herself she wouldn't set herself up to be hurt like that again. It was just too painful.

Needing to add a dash of reality to this picture-perfect evening, she asked, "Have you thought about how we're going to end all of this?"

Alex's brow creased. "Why would I think about something like that when we're having such a wonderful time?"

He had a good point, but fear overrode his words. "But eventually you're going to have to tell the press something when I go back to the States without you."

His fingers caressed her cheek. "Just for to-night, forget about the future and enjoy the mo-ment."

She wanted to, more than he knew. But this just wasn't right. They'd gotten caught up in the show they were putting on for the public. In re-ality, there was another woman in Alex's life.

The sobering reality propelled her away from him—needing a little space to resign herself to the fact that this evening, as beautiful as it was, couldn't happen. If they made love—if she laid her heart on the line—she couldn't bear to walk away from him. As it was, stepping on the plane now would be torture, but to know exactly what she'd be missing would be unbearable.

She stepped up to the rail to gaze out over the ocean as the sun was setting. Pink and pur-ple stretched across the horizon as a big ball of orange sank beneath the sea. The breeze tickled over her skin while the scent of salt filled her nose.

When she heard his footsteps approaching her, she tried to act normal—whatever that amounted to these days. "I've never seen anything so beautiful."

"I have." Alex's hands wrapped around her waist. "And I am holding her."

His compliment made her heart go tap-tap in her chest. She turned in his arms. "I'm sure you've been with much prettier women. What about Catherine? Shouldn't she be the one who is here with you?"

His brows gathered. "No, she shouldn't."

"But you're supposed to marry her."

"Is that what's bothering you?" When she nodded, he added, "Then stop worrying. I've called Catherine."

He did? Her heart took flight. "You told her about me?"

"Yes—"

Reese launched herself at him, smothering his words with a passionate kiss. Excitement and relief pumped through her veins. Her arms wrapped around his neck, pulling him close. There was nothing more she needed to hear. He'd told Catherine that they were together now. How could she have ever doubted him?

Reese hadn't known she could ever be this happy. The rush of feelings inside her was intense and they were fighting to get out. The time had come to quit holding back and trust him with her heart. Because if anyone was a good guy, it was Alex.

She pulled back and looked up at him. "Sometimes fantasies really do come true."

"Yes, they do."

He drew her back to him, the heat of his body permeating her dress. His lips pressed to hers. This time there was no hesitation in his touch. There was a deep need and a passionate desire in the way his mouth moved over hers. It lit a fire within her that mounted in intensity with each passing second.

Someone cleared his throat.

Reese jumped, pulling away from Alex's hold. She didn't know why she'd automatically assumed that they were alone. And that Alex had planned this as a romantic getaway for two.

Heat scorched her cheeks as she turned to face their visitor.

The butler stood at attention. "Sir, we need to know if you would like us to set up the meal inside or out."

Alex glanced at her. "It's your choice. Where would you like to dine?"

"Without the sun, the temps are dipping." She rubbed her arms, which were growing cold without his warmth next to them. "Would you mind if we eat inside?"

"Not at all. Would you like a fire lit?"

She glanced through the glass doors at the stone fireplace. The idea of sitting next to a crackling fire with Alex sounded perfectly romantic. "Yes, please."

Once the butler and small staff set about laying out the meal, Alex approached the fireplace mantel and retrieved a red plush Santa hat. "I think this will help set the mood."

She let him place the hat upon her head. "I guess it depends on what sort of mood you're creating."

"I'll let you wonder about that for now."

She spied another Santa hat on the mantel and

decided that the prince needed to have some fun with her. She tossed her beach bag on the couch and raced over to the mantel. With the other Santa hat in hand, she turned to Alex.

A smile lit up his face as he started shaking his head. "No way. I am not wearing that."

"This evening is all your creation. I think that you're more Santa today than I am. I'll be Santa's elf."

He stopped shaking his head as his eyes lit up with definite interest. "My elf, huh? I guess that means that you have to listen to me."

"I don't think so." She backed up but he followed her with a devilish look in his eyes. "Don't go getting any wild ideas."

He grabbed her by the sides and started tickling her. His fingers easily found her sensitive spots. She could barely breathe from all of the laughter. Though his magical fingers had stopped moving, he continued to hold her close. It felt so natural to be in his arms. Her arms draped over his shoulders as she leaned into him, trying to catch her breath.

His gaze met hers. "You know Santa left some packages over there under the tree for you."

She leaned her head to the side to see around his hulking form. "I can't believe I didn't see those before." She glanced back at him. "Are you sure they're for me?"

"I don't know. Were you a good girl this year?"

She nodded.

"Are you sure?"

She nodded again. "Can I open them now?"

"Not quite yet." When she stuck out her bottom lip, he added, "Surely you can wait until after dinner."

"But that's not what I'm pouting about. I only have one gift for you." She pulled away from him to move to the couch and reached in her beach bag. She removed a package all neatly wrapped in white tissue paper with a shiny red bow.

"You didn't have to get me anything."

"That's what makes it special. I wanted to. But I must warn you that it's nothing expensive or impressive."

"Anything you give me will be a thousand times more special than the most expensive wines or sports car."

"A sports car? So that's what you wanted Santa to bring you?"

He reached out for her hand and drew her to him, pulling her down on his lap. "Everything I want is here. You didn't have to get me a gift."

"I would have given it to you this morning at the gift exchange with your family, but I knew your family wouldn't understand the meaning behind it. And I didn't want to do anything that might be misconstrued by your father."

"That you don't have to worry about. Did you notice how well he's taken to you?"

"I know. What was up with that?"

"I told you that you had nothing to worry about by coming here. He really likes you—they all do. Most especially me."

By the glow of the firelight, they enjoyed soup and antipasto. Neither of them was that hungry after the large Christmas luncheon. This light fare was just perfect. And Alex was the perfect date as he kept her smiling and laughing with stories of adventures from his childhood.

"You were quite the daredevil back in the day," Reese surmised as she settled down on the rug and pillows in front of the fireplace. "Something tells me that the adventurous part of you is still lurking in there behind the prim and proper prince."

"You think so." He popped a bottle of Mirraccino's finest sparkling wine and the cork flew across the room. The contents bubbled over the top and he sucked up the overflow before it could make a mess.

"My point is proven." She laughed.

He poured them each a flute of the bubbly golden fluid and then held one out to her. She accepted it with a smile. This whole trip had been amazing and she had no doubt where the evening was headed.

"To the most beautiful woman I have ever known. May all of your wishes come true."

Their glasses clinked and before Reese even held the crystal stemware to her lips, a fluttery feeling filled her stomach. Her gaze met his hungry one. She took a sip of the sweet wine, but she barely noticed it as the cold liquid slid down her dry throat.

"You do know that we're all alone now?" He set aside his glass.

She set her wine next to his. Her gaze slipped down to his lips. They looked quite inviting.

"Does this mean that I get my Christmas present now?"

His voice came out unusually deep and gravelly. "That depends on what present you want to unwrap first."

She leaned toward him. "I think I'll start right here."

In the next breath her lips were covering his. When his arms wrapped around her, pulling her close, she could no longer deny that she had fallen for her very own Prince Charming. She loved Alex with every fiber of her being.

His hands encompassed her waist, pulling her to him. She willingly leaned into him. The sudden shift of her weight sent them falling back against the stack of pillows. She met him kiss for kiss, touch for touch. The fire crackled as Alex nuzzled her neck, causing her to laugh. She couldn't remember ever feeling so alive— so in love.

CHAPTER SEVENTEEN

A KNOCK SOUNDED.

Alex woke with a start. He squinted as the bright morning sun peeked in through the windows, catching him in the eyes. He glanced over finding Reese still breathing evenly as she lay snuggled beneath the pile of blankets. His thoughts filled with visions of her being in his arms. It had been the most amazing night of his life.

One kiss had led to another. One touch had led to another. And at last they'd ended up curled in front of the fireplace. He recalled how Reese's face had lit up with happiness. The sparkle in her big brown eyes had been his undoing. Her joy had filled a spot in him that he hadn't even known was empty.

He turned away from her sleeping figure and ran a hand over his hair, trying to will away the fogginess of sleep. This wasn't supposed to have happened. He hadn't meant for them to get in so deeply. Not yet. He still had so much to set straight with his family. And yet he couldn't deny that he cared deeply for Reese.

Another knock had him jumping to his feet. The fire had died out hours ago and a distinct chill hung in the air. He rushed to throw on his discarded and now wrinkled clothes. He moved silently across the hardwood floor to the front door.

His personal assistant stood at the door. The older man's face was creased with lines, but nothing in his very proper demeanor gave way to his thoughts of finding Alex in an awkward moment.

"Good morning, Guido." Alex kept his voice low so as not to wake Reese, since they'd gotten very little sleep. "What can I do for you?"

"I'm sorry to interrupt, sir." He also kept his voice to a whisper. "There's an urgent matter you must deal with at the palace."

Alex's chest tightened. He didn't like the sound of that. Thoughts of his papa's health and his brother's latest fiasco raced through his mind. "What is it?"

"There's another problem with a shipment at the port. I don't know the details. Only that you are requested to come immediately. I have a car waiting for you."

"Thank you. I'll be along soon."

"Yes, sir."

Alex closed the door gently. One of the problems with being a small nation was that the government was much more hands-on. He didn't understand why all of a sudden they were having endless problems at the port. And it didn't help matters that the problems seemed to concern a fleet of cargo ships owned by Catherine's father, who had been less than pleased with the last problem, involving a falsified manifest and a very greedy captain.

Alex didn't even want to guess what the harbormaster had uncovered this time. Dread coursed through his body. Still, there was no way around it. The only thing he could hope was that it was another shipping company.

"Who was at the door?" Reese's sleepy voice was deeper than normal and very sexy.

If only Alex didn't have important matters to

tend to, he'd spend a leisurely morning with her. But duty came first.

"It was a message from the palace that my attendance is needed."

Reese's eyes widened. "Is something wrong?"

"Nothing for you to worry about. Just a problem at the port." He slipped on his loafers and collected his things. "Take your time. There is food in the kitchen."

"But our presents. We didn't open them—"

"I'm sorry. There's no time now." He glanced at the fanciful packages beneath the tree. "It'll give us something to look forward to later."

"Unless we get distracted again." Her voice was still deep from sleep.

The sultry sound made him groan with frustration. "We'll get to them…eventually."

Her cheeks beamed a crimson hue, but that didn't stop her from teasing him. "I can't promise you that it'll be any time soon. I have plans for you."

"I'll hold you to your word." He leaned down and gave her a lingering kiss that made it almost painful to tear himself away from her. "I'll send the car back for you, but I have no idea how long I'll be."

* * *

How could someone be so unhappy when surrounded by such beauty?

Reese paced back and forth. It wasn't so much that she was unhappy...more like bored. Frustrated. Agitated. There was a whole dictionary full of words to describe her mood.

Sure, her palace suite was beautiful, from the high ceiling with its white, blue and gold polychrome tiles to the huge canopied bed. It was like sleeping in a very elegant museum—in fact, the entire palace was like something people only viewed in glossy magazines. It made her hesitant to touch anything for fear of breaking something.

She strolled over to the large window overlooking the sea. The sun was shining and the water was tranquil, unlike her mind, which could not rest. Her thoughts continually drifted back to Alex, as they had done so often since their very special evening together. Her cheeks warmed at the memory of how sweet and loving he'd been with her. It had been a perfect evening. So then why had Alex been gone the past twenty-four hours?

The only message she'd received from him had

come the prior evening, when he'd extended his apologies for missing dinner, claiming he had work to do. The note only made her even more curious about his whereabouts. What was so important? And why couldn't he deliver the message in person?

Unable to spend another lonely moment in her opulent suite, she threw on some old comfy jeans and a pink hoodie with a navy-blue New York logo emblazed over it. The clothes certainly weren't anywhere close to the fancy ones she'd been wearing since she'd arrived in Mirraccino, but she didn't feel a need to put on a show today. Besides, where she was headed there wouldn't be any paparazzi. And if there were, she was in no mood to care.

She headed for the private beach, hoping to clear her head—to figure out where she and Alex went from here. The sun warmed her back and helped her to relax. As for Alex, things there were complicated. It wasn't like being in a relationship with the guy next door. But she couldn't just walk away, either. The other night had drastically changed things. She'd given her heart to him.

A smile tugged at her face as she thought of Alex and how far they'd come. When she'd met him, she hadn't wanted a man in her life. She'd been unhappy, even though she hadn't realized it at the time. She'd had her eyes closed to her mother's progress, but Alex had helped her see things that were right in front of her. She'd learned to trust him and that she didn't have to be in control of everything all of the time. In fact, her daily calls to her mother revealed that The Willows was prospering without Reese's presence.

Her steps were light. It was as if she were tiptoeing along the fluffy white clouds dotting the sky. She was humming a little ditty to herself as she strolled down the beach, and then she spotted Alex. He was dressed in blue slacks and a blue button-up shirt with the sleeves rolled up. The breeze off the sea rustled his dark hair, scattering the strands. She was just about to call out to him when she got close enough to notice someone at his side. A woman. She was much shorter, with long dark hair that shimmered in the sun. They leaned toward each other as they laughed about something.

A sick feeling settled in the pit of Reese's stomach. She took a step backward. So this was why he'd been too busy to see her?

No. Alex wouldn't do something like this to her. He'd promised that she could trust him. And she'd given him her heart.

She dragged in a deep breath, hoping to calm her rising heart rate. She was jumping to conclusions. After all, he wasn't her father. He'd never leave her bed to go to another woman. *Have faith. Alex will make this right.*

Reese leveled her shoulders and forced her feet to move in the direction of the man she loved. She refused to be childish and jealous. There was a simple explanation to this. One that would make her feel foolish for jumping to conclusions. Maybe she was his cousin. Or the woman his brother had married. That must be it. He was comforting the woman and passing along a message from his brother.

"Good morning." Reese forced a smile on her face.

They both turned to her. Alex's brows lifted and the woman's eyes lit up as her gaze moved from Alex to Reese and back again. The woman's painted lips lifted into a smile.

Reese's radar was going off loud and clear, but she insisted on giving Alex a chance. "Beautiful morning, isn't it?"

Alex nodded. "Um…yes, it is." The surprise on his face slid behind a blank wall. "Reese, I would like you to meet Catherine."

"It is good to meet you." The woman's voice was warm and friendly. "You are the one helping, no?"

Catherine's English was tough to understand behind a heavy accent. "Yes…yes, I am."

But there was so much more to their relationship. Why did the woman seem a bit confused? Alex had said he'd told Catherine about her. An uneasy feeling settled in her stomach. She'd once again let her naivety get her into trouble. She should have asked him exactly what he'd told the woman. Because it obviously wasn't that he loved Reese. That much was clear.

Catherine smiled and held out her hand. "I would like us to be friends, no?"

Reese didn't have much choice but to force a smile and extend her hand. The sunshine gleamed off the pink sapphire, reminding her of the heated kiss she'd shared with Alex when he'd given it to her. What would Catherine make of the ring?

She searched the woman's face for some hint of hostility or jealousy, but she didn't detect any. The woman truly appeared to be kind and outgoing. What was Reese missing? Had Alex duped them both?

Not understanding any of this, she turned a questioning look to Alex. But his gaze didn't meet hers. Except for the slight tic in his cheek, there was nothing in his outward appearance to let her know that he was uncomfortable with this meeting.

Oblivious to the undercurrents running between Alex and Reese, Catherine said, "You help Alex with paparazzi, no?" The woman's voice was soft and gentle. When Reese nodded, the woman continued to speak. "You are a good woman. He is lucky to have you."

What could she say to that? Though it killed her to exchange pleasantries when all she wanted to do was confront Alex, she uttered, "Thank you."

Alex cleared his throat. "Catherine and I were headed back inside. I have a meeting to attend. Would you care to join us?"

There was no warmth in his voice. No acknowledgement that they were anything more than casual acquaintances. Just the cool politeness of a politician.

"Yes, join us. I want to know about you and New York." Catherine's eyes reflected her sincerity.

With determined reserve, Reese maintained a cool outward appearance. "I think I'll stay out here. I'd like to stretch my legs. One can only be cooped up for so long."

Reese turned to Alex and bit back an impolite comment. There was no way she could be rude to Alex in front of this woman. As much as she wanted to dislike Catherine, she couldn't; she appeared to be a genuinely nice person. In another universe, Reese could imagine being fast friends with Catherine. But not here—not today.

Reese could only presume that the woman didn't know what had transpired between her and Alex the other night. And there was no way she would be the one to tell her. That was Alex's problem.

What she had to say to him—and there was a lot—would have to wait. She didn't need this woman knowing what a fool she'd made of herself, falling for a prince far outside her league.

A look of relief crossed Alex's face. "Then we'll leave you to enjoy the day."

He extended his arm to Catherine, who turned to Reese. "Nice to meet you. We talk later."

"Nice to meet you, too." Reese couldn't believe how hard it was to say those words without choking on her own tongue.

She stood there watching the departing couple. Catherine's head momentarily leaned against Alex's arm, as though she knew him well—very well. The thought slashed into Reese's heart. She was the odd man out.

It wasn't until they turned the corner and headed up the steps toward the palace that Reese realized she'd been holding her breath. She was afraid to breathe out—afraid the balled-up emotions inside her would come tumbling out. She blinked repeatedly, clearing her blurring vision. She wanted to believe that this was some sort of nightmare and she'd wake up soon. Because it just couldn't be possible that she'd been duped into being the other woman.

Her stomach lurched. Her hands wrapped

around her midsection as she willed away the waves of nausea. After all of the days and nights of wondering how her father's lover could have carried on an affair—now Reese was in those very uncomfortable shoes. And she hated it.

She started walking down the beach with no destination in mind. Her only thought was to get away. Her steps came faster. Throughout the whole drama with her father's death and finding out that he'd siphoned off their savings, she'd had a hard time believing her mother hadn't known anything about it. How could she not?

Looking back on it, there had been so many clues—so many things that didn't add up. She'd ended up harboring angry feelings toward her mother for allowing all of that to happen to them by turning a blind eye to her father's activities. But now Reese had more compassion for the situation her mother had been in. When you love someone, you trust them.

Reese stopped walking, drawing one quick breath after the other. She glanced around, realizing she'd ended up back at the bungalow. She hadn't realized she'd wandered so far down the beach.

Her legs were tired and her face was warm from the sun, but it was the aching loss in her chest that had the backs of her eyes stinging. She refused to dissolve into a puddle of tears. She wouldn't stop living just because she'd once again let herself be duped by a man. The memory of Alex and Catherine arm in arm and with their heads together, laughing, was emblazoned on her memory. How could she have trusted him?

With renewed anger, she started off for the palace. This fairy tale had come to an end. And like Cinderella, it was time to trade in her gowns for a vacuum and a day planner.

She'd reached the bottom of the steps up the cliff when she spotted Alex sitting there. He didn't notice her at first and she paused, not sure she was up for this confrontation. Still, it was best to meet it head-on and get it over with. She didn't want any lingering *what if*s or *should have*s. This would end things cleanly.

Leveling her shoulders, she headed straight for him. When he saw her, he got to his feet and met her halfway. Lines bracketed his eyes and his face looked as though he'd aged a few years. Was he that worried that she'd blow things for him with Catherine? She took a bit of satisfaction in knowing that he was stressed. It was the least he could feel after he'd used her without any thought to her feelings.

"Reese, you had me worried. You didn't tell anyone where you were going."

She crossed her arms and narrowed her gaze on him. "I'm sure you were too busy to be worried about me."

"That's not fair. You know I care."

"Was Catherine the reason you took off after we spent the night together?" *Right after I'd given you my heart. When I'd at last trusted you.*

"No. I told you there was a problem at the port."

Reese crossed her arms and hitched up a hip. "So what's she doing here?"

"She knew I wanted to speak with her, and since a problem had arisen with one of the ships her father owns, she flew in. I knew nothing of her arrival until last evening."

Reese wasn't about to assume anything this time around. "Does Catherine know how you spent the other night?"

V-shaped lines etched between his brows. "Of course she doesn't know. What kind of man do you think I am? I don't go around discussing personal things."

"The kind who likes to keep a woman on the side like a spare suit or an extra pair of shoes." Her voice quavered with anger. "Is that what I am to you?"

"No, of course not." His blue eyes pleaded with her to believe him, but she was too worked up to be swayed so easily. "But you don't understand. I can't just blurt out to Catherine that I have feelings for you."

"Why?"

He glanced down and rubbed the back of his neck. "Because I won't hurt her like that. She deserves better."

Reese heard the words he hadn't spoken, louder and clearer than anything else. He cared about Catherine. Those powerful words blindsided Reese. They knocked into her full force, stealing the breath from her lungs. She stumbled back.

He had real feelings for Catherine.

Reese's teeth sank into her lower lip, holding in a backlash of anger and a truckload of pain. How stupid could she have been? Catherine oozed money and culture. The woman was a perfect match for a prince. Reese glanced down at her faded jeans and worn sweatshirt. She'd laugh at the comparison, but she was afraid that it'd come out in sobs. She swallowed down her emotions.

"We don't have anything left to say to each other. You should go to her—to your future fiancée."

"You're spinning this out of control. Catherine has nothing to do with you and me."

"Yes, she does. She has everything to do with this. You care about her."

Not me!

A sob caught in the back of her throat. A piercing pain struck her heart, causing a burning sensation at the backs of her eyes. She loved him, but he didn't feel the same way. She clenched her hands, fighting to keep her pain bottled up. She refused to let him see just how deeply he'd hurt her.

"Let me explain. We can work this out—"

"No, we can't." Her nails dug into her palms as she struggled to maintain her composure. "Do you know how much this hurts? It's killing me to stand here. To be so close to you and yet so far away."

He lifted his head and stared up at the blue sky for a moment, as though coming up with a rebuttal. "You don't understand. I do care about her. But I don't love her."

Reese heard the sincerity in his voice and saw the pleading look in his eyes. Maybe he hadn't set out to make her the other woman, but that didn't change the fact that three was a crowd. And she wasn't going to stick around to make a further fool of herself.

"I'm leaving."

Alex reached out, grabbing her arm. "Don't leave like this."

She spun around so fast his eyes widened in surprise. "Why not? What reason do I have to stay?" Her throat burned as the raw words came tumbling out. "Did you end things with Catherine? Did you tell your family the marriage is off?"

He held her gaze. "It's not that easy. Her father is very influential. If he pulls his business from Mirraccino, it'll have a devastating ripple effect on the country's economy. But you must know that I have never made any promises to her. It's all a business arrangement—my duty."

"You're forgetting I saw you two together. You aren't strangers."

"You're right. Catherine and I have been friends since we were kids. But I swear it has never gone further than that—"

"Stop." She wasn't going to let his smooth tongue and convincing words confuse her. "The fact is you can't have us both. It's time you choose between your duty and your desires."

She stood there pleading with her eyes for him to choose her—to choose love. But as the strained silence stretched on, her hopes were dashed. She had no choice but to accept that his duty to the crown would always come first. She might have fallen in love with him, but obviously it was a one-way street.

A tear dripped onto her cheek and she quickly dashed it away. "I—I have some packing to do."

She pulled her shoulders back and moved past him with determined steps. It was time to make a hasty exit before she dissolved into a disgusting puddle of self-pity. And she couldn't let that happen. Her heart was already in tattered ruins. The only thing she had left was her pride.

Alex jogged over to stand in front of her. "Give me time to sort things out."

"You can have all of the time in the world. I'm leaving." Then as an afterthought, she slipped off the pink sapphire and tossed it at him. "And I won't be needing this any longer."

She turned and strode up the beach…alone.

CHAPTER EIGHTEEN

ALEX PLACED THE STORYBOOK Reese had given him for Christmas next to his suitcase.

He probably shouldn't have opened it without her. But after she'd left he'd been so lonely without her that he needed a tangible connection.

He stared down at the hardback copy of *How the Grinch Stole Christmas*. Was she sending him a message? Did she really think his heart was three sizes too small? Probably. And he couldn't blame her for thinking so. He'd made a total mess of things.

Since the day she'd left him standing on the beach, he'd barely slept. He couldn't wipe the devastated look on her face from his mind. For all of his trying to stay aloof and objective, he'd fallen head over heels in love with her.

It wasn't until he'd tried explaining his relationship with Catherine and his family's expectations for him to Reese that he realized he'd spent his entire life being the perfect prince and honor bound to the crown. And he just couldn't do it any longer—not at the expense of his love for the one woman who made him want more than his position within the monarchy, the woman who made him believe that without love, he had nothing.

Now the time had come for him to make his needs a priority, even if they didn't coincide with the family's view of an acceptable life for a prince. At last, he fully understood what his brother had gone through with his brief marriage. And from the look of Demetrius, he really did love that woman. Now Alex wondered if his brother would ever have a chance at true happiness.

However, Alex wasn't the crown prince. He wasn't held to such high standards. He'd made his decision and now he didn't have time to waste. After a few phone calls to make the necessary arrangements, Alex went to meet with the king.

Papa was having breakfast with his brother and Catherine. Alex came to a stop at the end of the formal dining table, more certain than ever that he was doing the right thing.

"You're late." The king pointed at a chair. "Join us."

"I don't have time. I have something urgent I must do."

"I would think Catherine's presence would be your priority."

Alex glanced at Catherine. He'd spoken to her last night and explained how he had planned to do his duty, no matter what was asked of him, but somewhere along the way, he'd lost his heart to a beautiful firecracker from New York. And he just couldn't pass up his one chance to be truly happy. Catherine was happy for him. She had a secret of her own. She was in love with someone, too, but she had been reluctant to do anything about it. Now both Catherine and he could be happy.

She nodded at him, as though giving him encouragement to keep going. He hoped someday he, Reese and Catherine could all be friends. But he had to win back Reese's heart first.

"Catherine and I have spoken and we're not getting engaged. Not now. Not ever."

The king's gaze narrowed. "Alexandro, we've discussed this and it has been decided that you'll marry Catherine. And it's high time that you do it."

Alex shook his head. "From now on, I'll be making my own decisions about who I marry." He made direct eye contact with the king. "I'll not let you bully me into giving up the woman that I love like you did with Demetrius."

The king's fork clattered against the plate. "I did no such thing. Your brother and that woman decided to part ways of their own accord."

Alex didn't believe it. Demetrius was too distraught to have dumped his wife. But when Alex turned to his twin, his brother nodded his head.

"It's true. Papa didn't split us up."

The king sat back and crossed his arms. Alex wasn't about to give up. This was far too important—Reese was far too important.

Alex continued to stand at attention the way he used to do when he was young and in a world of trouble. "You should also know that I'm not going to drop everything in my life to cover for the latest scandal to strike the family. I have my own life to lead. And my priority is seeking the forgiveness of the woman I love. I've put my duty ahead of her since the day I met her. Now it's time that she comes first."

His brother's mouth gaped. Too bad he hadn't been able to make such a bold move. But the crown prince didn't have as many options.

Everyone grew quiet, waiting for the king's reaction. What would he say? Alex didn't honestly know. The breath caught in his throat as he waited, hoping the king wouldn't disown him.

His papa made direct eye contact with him. "I've done a lot of thinking these past few weeks. Though there are legitimate reasons for a strategic marriage, perhaps there's another way to strike up the necessary allegiances. Who am I to deny my sons a chance to know love like your mother and I shared?"

Alex had to be certain he'd heard the king correctly. "You approve of Reese."

The king's silver head nodded. "When you are in New York, make sure you invite your new princess to the palace for the winter ball. It will be the perfect place to properly introduce her to everyone."

Alex truly liked the idea of escorting Reese to the ball. He just hoped she would find it in her heart to forgive him. "I'll most definitely invite her."

Alex didn't spare any time making his way to the private airstrip. With the king's blessing, he knew that he could now have his family and the woman he loved—if she would forgive him.

CHAPTER NINETEEN

THIS HAS TO WORK.

Alex stared blindly out the car window. Large, fluffy snowflakes fell, limiting visibility. Aside from the snow, his return to New York City was so different than his last visit. This time he was surrounded by his security detail and instead of a wild taxi ride he was settled in the comfortable backseat of a black town car with diplomatic tags. There was no looking over his shoulder. This time it didn't matter who knew he was in town.

His only goal for being here was to win back Reese's trust—her love.

The car tires crunched over the snow. He glanced out the window at the passing houses. They were getting close. His gut tightened. Normally when he had an important speech, he'd make notes and settle most of what he'd say ahead of time. This time, he didn't know what he'd say. He didn't even know if he'd get past the front door.

The car tires spun a bit as the car eased into the driveway. Alex pulled on his leather gloves. Before the car pulled to a full stop, Alex had the back door open. He took the porch steps two at a time.

His foot had just touched the porch when the door swung open. It was Reese. Her long hair was swept back in a smooth ponytail. Her bangs fell smoothly over her forehead. Her eyes widened as she took in his appearance. "What are you doing here?"

He might have been prepared for the winter weather, but he wasn't prepared for the hard edge in her voice.

"Hello, Reese. You forgot your Christmas presents."

Her eyes grew round. "You flew all the way here to give me some presents?"

"And I thought we should talk—"

"No. Take your presents and go away. We said everything that needed to be said." She waved him away. When he didn't move, she added, "We were a publicity stunt. Nothing more. Now go home to Catherine."

He refused to be deterred. One way or another, she'd hear him out. "I am here on a matter of great importance."

"That's too bad. I'm on my way out. I don't have time to talk."

"Then let me give you a ride." He moved aside so she could see his hired car. Other women he'd met would swoon at this opportunity. But Reese wasn't other women. She wouldn't be easily swayed. But she was most definitely worth the effort.

When he sensed she was about to turn him down, he added, "Either let me take you or expect to see me waiting here when you return."

"You wouldn't."

He arched a brow. There was hardly a thing he wouldn't do to win her back.

She sighed and rolled her eyes. "Fine. If this is what it takes to get rid of you, let's get it over with."

Her pointed words stabbed at his chest. He knew he'd hurt her, but he'd been hoping with time that she would have become more reasonable—more understanding. So much for that wishful thinking. He would have to do a lot of pleading if he was ever going to get her to forgive him. And he wasn't well versed in apologies. Good thing he was a quick learner.

He waved away the driver, getting the door for her himself. Reese was one of the strongest people he knew. She'd held together her family after her father's betrayal. Not everyone could do that. Now he had to hope that she had enough compassion in her heart for him—to realize that he'd learned from his mistakes.

Reese gave the driver a Manhattan address before turning to Alex. "I hope you really do have something important on your mind. Otherwise you're wasting both our time."

"Trust me. This is very important." She arched a disbelieving brow at him, but he didn't let that deter him. "Do you mind me asking where we're headed?"

"An art school. I've enrolled and this is the first class of the semester. I'm working on my graphic art."

"But what about The Willows? How do you have time to do everything?"

She leaned her head back against the black leather upholstery and stared up at the ceiling. "When I got back from Mirraccino, I found that you were right." Her face contorted into a frown as she made the admission. "I'd been hovering over my mother too much. While I was gone, she handled this place. She regained her footing."

"That's great news. And now you can follow your dreams."

Reese nodded. "It seems my mother and Mr.— erm, Howard are officially dating, too."

"And how does that make you feel?"

She shrugged. "Happy, I guess. After all, it isn't like she owed anything to the memory of my father. So if Howard makes her happy, I'm good with that. Now what brings you here?"

He removed an official invitation with the royal seal from the inner pocket of his black wool coat. He held it out to her. When their fingers brushed, a jolt rushed up his arm and settled in his chest. She quickly pulled back.

He cleared his throat. "Before you open that, I have a few things to say."

She glanced out the window into the snowy afternoon. "Make it quick. We're almost there."

"Reese, I want you to know how sorry I am for not being more up front about my situation with Catherine. I had mentioned you to her on the phone, but I didn't bring up that we were intimately involved. I wasn't sure of Catherine's feelings and didn't want to announce that I wasn't going through with the engagement over the phone."

Reese nailed him with an astonished stare. "So it was better to keep your fiancée in the dark?"

"She was never my fiancée. Not like you're thinking. I never proposed to her. I never loved her. We are friends. Nothing more. In fact, when I told her that you and I were involved, she told me that she was happy to be released from the arrangement because she had fallen in love with someone."

Reese's brows rose. "You're serious."

"Yes. Catherine was as relieved as I was to call off the marriage."

"I bet your family didn't take it well."

"The king respected my decision."

Reese twisted around to look at him face-to-face. "You're really serious? You stood up and told everyone about us?"

"Yes, I did. I realized that I'd let my sense of duty take over my life. I told them that I wouldn't be on call twenty-four-seven to cover up any scandals. You had to come first."

Her eyes opened wide. "You really said that?"

He nodded, reaching out to take her hands in his. "Please believe me. I know I messed up in the past, but I won't let that happen again. No more secrets."

His gaze probed hers, looking for some sign that he was getting through to her. But in a blink her surprise slid behind a solid wall of indifference. Was he wrong about her? Didn't she feel the same as him?

Before he could think of something else to say to convince her to give him another chance, the car pulled to a stop in front of a building.

She grabbed her backpack from the seat. "This is where I get out."

"Can I wait for you? We can talk some more. I know we can work this out."

"No. You've said what you've come here to say. Now please go."

She got out of the car and closed the door with a resounding thud. His chest ached as he watched her walk away. He raked his fingers through his hair and pulled on the short strands as he fought off the urge to go after her.

What had she just done?

Panic clutched Reese's chest. She rushed over to the building, heedless of the coating of snow on the sidewalk. She yanked open the door of the arts building and hustled inside with no real destination in mind. It wasn't until she was away from the wall of windows and out of sight of the car that she stopped and leaned against the wall. It was then that she let out a pent-up breath.

Had she lost her mind?

Had she really just turned down an honest-to-goodness prince?

But it wasn't a royal prince that she loved. It was plain Alex—a living, breathing, imperfect human—the same person who'd hurt her. Alex just happened to come with an impressive title and hung his coat in an amazing palace. But those physical things weren't enough to sway her decision.

The backs of her eyes stung and she blinked, re-fusing to give in to tears. He'd said all of the right things. Why couldn't she let down her guard? Why couldn't she give him another chance?

She glanced at the large metal clock on the far wall. She had five minutes until her class started. She'd been hoping that going back to school would fill the empty spot in her life—help her forget—but nothing could wipe away the memories of Alex.

Part of her wanted to run back out the door and into his arms. The other part of her said it just wasn't right. Something was missing.

She glanced down at the envelope he'd handed her in the car. Her name was scrolled over the front of the heavy parchment. The royal seal of Mirraccino was stamped onto the back. Curiosity poked at her.

Her finger slipped into the opening in the flap and she ripped along the fold. Inside was an invitation that read:

King Ferdinando of Mirraccino formally invites you to the Royal Winter Ball. The grand fete will take place at the royal palace on Saturday, the seventh of March at six o'clock. The honor of your presence is requested.

Reese stared at the invitation for a moment, stunned that she was holding an invitation to a royal ball. A deep, weary sigh passed her lips. When she went to put the invitation in her purse, it slipped from her fingers and fluttered to the floor.

She bent over to snatch it up when she noticed some handwriting on the back of the invite. She pulled it closer.

Reese, I love you with every fiber of my being. Please be my princess at the ball.
Alex

He loved her!

Those were the words she'd been waiting to hear.

Her lips lifted and her heart pounded. In that moment, the pieces all fell into place. She loved him and he loved her.

In the next breath, the smile slipped from her lips. She'd sent him away. Was it too late? Was he gone for good?

She took off running for the door. He had to be there. He couldn't have left yet.

Please let him still be here.

Practically knocking over a couple of young guys coming through the door, she yelled an apology over her shoulder and kept moving. She stepped onto the sidewalk and stopped.

The black town car was gone. For the first time ever, Alex had finally done as she'd asked. Why now? Tears pricked her eyes.

And then she saw it. The black town car. That had to be the one. It was approaching the end of the block and had on its turn signal.

She had to stop him. Not worrying about the ice or snow, she set off running after the car. She couldn't give up. She was so close to having the man she loved.

The car came to a stop at the intersection. She called out to Alex, not that he would hear her. Then the brake lights went out and the car surged forward. Reese's chest burned as she called out one last time to him.

Then the bright brake lights flashed on and Alex emerged from the back. He sent her a questioning look before he set off toward her with open arms. She rushed toward him with the intention of never leaving his embrace.

After he held her for a moment, he took a step back so they could make eye contact. "I don't understand. What changed your mind?"

"You did."

"But how? When you got out of the car, you were so certain."

She held up the invitation. "What you wrote here said everything I needed to know."

His eyes closed as he sighed. "I was so worried about apologizing that I totally forgot to tell you the most important part. Reese, since I've known you my heart has grown three sizes because it's so full of love for you. I promise I'll tell you every day for the rest of our lives."

She smiled up at him. "Why don't you start now?"

"I love you."

"I love you, too."

EPILOGUE

Two months later...

PRINCE ALEXANDRO CASTANAVO stared across the hallway at Reese. He'd never seen anyone so beautiful. She stole his breath away. And the best part was she was beautiful inside and out. After they'd spent the past couple of weeks at the palace, no one in Mirraccino could deny that Reese would make a generous and kind princess.

Tonight's ball was for the residents of Mirraccino. With it being between growing seasons, this was the nation's chance to celebrate the past year and the royal family's chance to mingle with the citizens—to bring the island together.

And it was Alex's chance to introduce them to the queen of his heart. They were going to love her as much as he did—well, maybe not that much, but pretty close.

He approached and offered his arm to her. She

smiled up at him and his heart thumped. How had he ended up being the luckiest man alive?

"May I escort you into the ballroom?"

Reese grabbed the skirt of her royal-blue-and-silver gown and curtsied. Her eyes sparkled with mischief.

"Why yes, Your Highness."

"You know, I like the sound of that." He couldn't help but tease her back and he put on a serious expression. "Perhaps I'll have you address me as Your Highness all the time."

Reese's mouth gaped. "You wouldn't."

He smiled. "I'm teasing you. I love you the way you are, strong and feisty. I'd never try to change that about you."

Before he could say more, they were summoned inside the ballroom to be announced.

"His Royal Highness, Prince Alexandro Castanavo, and Her Ladyship, Miss Reese Harding."

Before they could be ushered into the crowd, Alex held up his hand, pausing the procession. "If you all will allow me a moment, I have something very special to share."

A hush fell over the crowded room. He fished a black velvet box from his pocket. He was surprised the box had any material left after he'd looked inside at least a couple hundred times trying to decide if it was the right ring for Reese. In the end, he couldn't imagine her with any other ring.

He dropped to one knee and heard Reese's swift intake of breath. He lifted his head and smiled at her, hoping to reassure her. Still, she sent him a wide-eyed gaze.

He took her now trembling hand in his and he realized that perhaps his idea to share this very special moment with everyone he cared about had been a miscalculation. But he was on bended knee now and the room was so quiet that he could hear the beating of his own heart.

"Reese, would you do me the honor of being my princess today and for all of the days of my life?"

Her eyes sparkled with tears of joy as she vigorously nodded. "Yes, I will."

He stood tall and removed the ring from the box. His hands weren't too steady as he slipped the five-carat pink sapphire surrounded by sixty-four diamond side stones onto her finger.

"You kept it." She held up her hand to look at it.

"I thought the ring had a special meaning for us. You aren't disappointed, are you?"

She held up her hand to admire the engagement ring. "I love it!" Her warm gaze moved to him. "But not as much as I love you."

* * * * *

MILLS & BOON®
Large Print – February 2015

AN HEIRESS FOR HIS EMPIRE
Lucy Monroe

HIS FOR A PRICE
Caitlin Crews

COMMANDED BY THE SHEIKH
Kate Hewitt

THE VALQUEZ BRIDE
Melanie Milburne

THE UNCOMPROMISING ITALIAN
Cathy Williams

PRINCE HAFIZ'S ONLY VICE
Susanna Carr

A DEAL BEFORE THE ALTAR
Rachael Thomas

THE BILLIONAIRE IN DISGUISE
Soraya Lane

THE UNEXPECTED HONEYMOON
Barbara Wallace

A PRINCESS BY CHRISTMAS
Jennifer Faye

HIS RELUCTANT CINDERELLA
Jessica Gilmore

MILLS & BOON®
Large Print – March 2015

A VIRGIN FOR HIS PRIZE
Lucy Monroe

THE VALQUEZ SEDUCTION
Melanie Milburne

PROTECTING THE DESERT PRINCESS
Carol Marinelli

ONE NIGHT WITH MORELLI
Kim Lawrence

TO DEFY A SHEIKH
Maisey Yates

THE RUSSIAN'S ACQUISITION
Dani Collins

THE TRUE KING OF DAHAAR
Tara Pammi

THE TWELVE DATES OF CHRISTMAS
Susan Meier

AT THE CHATEAU FOR CHRISTMAS
Rebecca Winters

A VERY SPECIAL HOLIDAY GIFT
Barbara Hannay

A NEW YEAR MARRIAGE PROPOSAL
Kate Hardy

MILLS & BOON®

Why shop at millsandboon.co.uk?

Each year, thousands of romance readers find their perfect read at millsandboon.co.uk. That's because we're passionate about bringing you the very best romantic fiction. Here are some of the advantages of shopping at www.millsandboon.co.uk:

* **Get new books first**—you'll be able to buy your favourite books one month before they hit the shops

* **Get exclusive discounts**—you'll also be able to buy our specially created monthly collections, with up to 50% off the RRP

* **Find your favourite authors**—latest news, interviews and new releases for all your favourite authors and series on our website, plus ideas for what to try next

* **Join in**—once you've bought your favourite books, don't forget to register with us to rate, review and join in the discussions

Visit **www.millsandboon.co.uk**
for all this and more today!